HE BEGAN TO STROKE HER ARM

. . . and her neck . . . and her cheek. "Don't be afraid," he murmured, again and again. He put his other hand on her hip.

A charge, more intense than the lightning outside, went through her. She turned slowly—as if drawn by a magnet—and raised her lips. He kissed her gently. Once. Twice. Three times. The fourth kiss was not gentle, and the fifth drained the breath from her lungs.

Simultaneously their hands dropped to their sides. He was the first to speak: "I'm sorry."

"Are you? I can't honestly say that I am."

"You're not?" He chuckled. "Then I'm not. I had planned not to let myself . . . I should stay away from you. I *must* stay away from you."

"Because of Rick?" she asked.

"He's one reason . . ."

"There are others?"

He didn't answer. They sat in silence as the thunder rumbled off into the distance. . . .

St. Martin's Paperbacks Titles by LouAnn Gaeddert

PERFECT STRANGERS

EVER AFTER

ROSES AFTER RAIN

Roses After Rain

LouAnn Gaeddert

ST. MARTIN'S PAPERBACKS

Portions of this novel have previously appeared in *Good Housekeeping* under the title "The Searching Heart."

ROSES AFTER RAIN

Cover photograph by George Kerrigan.

ISBN: 0-312-92685-5

Printed in the United States of America

St. Martin's Paperbacks edition/March 1992

10 9 8 7 6 5 4 3 2 1

Chapter One

MEG Bower bit her lip and grasped the watering can firmly with both hands as she lifted it to a fern hanging in the window. Still some of the water splashed down on the sword plant sitting on the sill below. Why, she asked herself, should she feel jittery about meeting Rick's aunt and his brother and his old friends? Once upon a time, most social situations had made her nervous. Not now. Now she was engaged to marry Rick who would be by her side. She wasn't anxious, she was excited.

When she had watered the last plant in her window, she draped a plastic-wrapped dress over her shoulder, grabbed her tote bag and stroked a wooden walrus on the shelf near the door. The walrus was a gift from Rick. She ran out of the apartment and down the hall to the elevator.

Rick was waiting in a white subcompact car parked in the bus stop in front of her building. He grinned a welcome as he leaned over to open the curbside door. When she had stashed her tote and dress in the back, she leaned toward him. He kissed her tenderly.

"Sorry I'm late," she whispered as she leaned toward him again. A foghorn toot! They sprang apart and looked back at the bus that had pulled to the curb behind them.

Rick patted her knee and inched the car out into the traffic lane. "For you, beautiful lady, I'd wait a century on a bed of nails."

She laughed and fastened her seat belt while he drove down Manhattan's Second Avenue and turned right on Seventy-fifth Street and left on Fifth Avenue. "Take special note of that building," he said, waving toward a small ornate building wedged between two towering slabs. He made another left turn and then a right. Eventually they were on FDR Drive heading north.

She tried to keep a picture of the building in her mind. Why, she wondered, had he negotiated all of those one-way streets to show her that particular building? True, they needed a place to live together. On Fifth Avenue? A picture of the shoddy trailer that had been her childhood home flitted through her brain and she began to hum the tune that went with a song about walking down Fifth Avenue.

"So what did you think of that building on Fifth Avenue, Meg?"

"Could you recognize the tune I was humming?"

"Tune?" he asked, bewildered.

"From *Easter Parade.* Remember when Fred and Judy in tramp costumes sing 'We're a Couple of Swells'? I assume you showed me that building because you'd like to live there. I wouldn't; I'm not ready for Fifth Avenue, unless there's a Fifth Avenue in the Bronx." She laughed and kissed his cheek. "Besides, that little building looks like a midget squeezed between two giants."

"A media buyer in my office is buying there. Three rooms for only two-fifty. Maintenance isn't bad, either."

"Two hundred and fifty thousand dollars for three rooms that are surely dark?" Meg was appalled. And then she laughed. What difference did it make how much the apartment cost?

"I asked him to let me know if a similar apartment came on the market," Rick said stiffly.

"Oh Rick, why?"

"Don't tell me you wouldn't like to live across the street from Central Park."

"I suppose I would, but there's one wee problem. Dare I mention it? It's green and filthy and absolutely necessary. I have no assets, only debts. But you know that." She paused and then giggled. "Have you been holding out on me? Did you win the lottery? Inherit a fortune? Are you an oil-rich sheik in disguise?"

"Better. I have a brilliant future—and so do you." He grinned without taking his eyes from the traffic in front of him. "If I land the Webster account, I'll be in the soaring mode. And you, my dear Attorney Bower, have just won an important case. You are rushing straight down the path to a partnership. How was the party? Bet you all had one grand time celebrating your victory."

"Actually, I left early."

"Why?" He sounded stunned.

"Everyone was running around thumping backs

and shouting congratulations to one another. And gloating over the gloom in the enemy camp. We were like high school kids who had just won the big game."

"So what's wrong with that? Some of your people had been working on the case for years. They had a right to gloat for one night. I'm sure they gloated discreetly."

Meg leaned back against the headrest. "I'm just glad it's over," she said, sighing.

"So am I, love. I've hardly seen you the last six weeks. If we'd had an apartment, we could at least have had breakfast together. You're tired, aren't you? So close your eyes and sleep for an hour or two?"

"You work hard, too." She transferred a kiss from her finger to his cheek, yawned and slid down on her spine.

When the car stopped and then made a sharp left-hand turn, she stretched and opened her eyes. They were in a town studded with large clapboard houses on broad lawns.

"Hello, Sleeping Beauty," he said. "Time to wake up. We're in Great Barrington."

"Good afternoon," she mumbled, stifling a yawn. "Sorry I've been such a social dog. The least I could have done was to try to entertain you while you were driving. Is there time for me to make amends? Want me to sing?"

"We're almost there, fortunately. The wedding's at four in the Stonefield church."

"And then?"

"A quote, buffet supper, end quote, at the new home of the bride and groom."

"Why the quote, end quote?"

"Because the so-called buffet supper will actually be a picnic—fried chicken, potato salad, maybe ham, maybe roast beef, deviled eggs . . ."

"I love deviled eggs."

"Piet says the new house is one of those modular boxes set down in the middle of what used to be Jerry's grandfather's pasture." Rick shook his head and sighed. "Jerry and I sure had some grand times on his grandfather's farm. We built a bridge and a hut and played baseball. Haven't seen old Jerry much since high school. He's an engineer. Laura's a nurse. Hot stuff by Stonefield standards."

"Hot stuff by almost anyone's standards, Rick. Have you known the bride forever, too?"

"Practically. She was the pesty kid sister of a guy in our class. Buck teeth. Skinned knees."

"Poor Laura." Meg's sympathy was genuine. She had been the tallest girl in her class, and angular. Her hair, red then, had been stick-straight. "So tell me about your brother. His name's Peter? What does he do for a living?"

"His name is pronounced Pete, but it's the Dutch version, P-I-E-T. He's a sort of jack-of-all-trades. Two years older than I."

"Tell me more." Meg combed her short hair, auburn now, back away from her face, and then flipped one side forward. "A brother of yours would have to be bright."

"He must have an average IQ, but he was a poor student and he never went to college. He's sweet natured. He'd give you his last dollar if you asked for it, or repair your car or put a new roof on your house. Piet and Aunt Hat and I are giving the bride and groom a landscape job because Piet says that's what they need. Aunt Hat says that Piet just looks at plants and they grow. Our father had the same talent."

"Piet sounds like a dear. Tell me more. Is he married?"

"No. He was within two days of the altar once but the girl broke it off. She decided she'd rather stay in college and find herself a college man."

"She waited until two days before the wedding to decide that?"

Rick shrugged. "Don't waste your worry on Piet. He's good-looking; he'll find a sweet little home-body type one of these days." He made a sharp right turn into a narrow black-topped road curving between tall trees.

"He can't be as handsome as you." Meg studied his profile. Rick was the quintessential Dutchman, Hans Brinker grown to maturity. Straight blond hair, slightly long. Bright blue eyes. Fair skin. He would have been pretty if his nose had not been a little long and his lips had not been firm and thin. He was not quite six feet tall, three inches taller than she, and slim.

"We'll be the best-looking couple at the wedding, and the most successful." Rick wasn't bragging, just stating the facts as he saw them. They were an attractive couple. Meg knew that, and yet she didn't.

She had grown up thinking of herself as brainy, neat, and homely. All through college and law school she had dressed in jeans and worn her hair in a skimpy ponytail. She had reported to work at Savage, Smith, and Spencer with her hair pulled back into a neat bun and wearing a navy blue linen suit so expensive that she had imagined her credit card turning into nervous jelly.

A week later Meg's butterfly self had begun to emerge from its cocoon when she rented a room from a stranger named Blythe who became her fairy godmother. An assistant fashion editor, Blythe was eager to preach the gospel of flair to the heathen drab, Meg still remembered the panic she had felt as her long hair began to litter the floor of a chic shop on Madison Avenue and her shock when she received the bill, sixty-seven dollars *plus* tip! She also remembered the pleasure of slipping into the first bargain dress Blythe had brought home to her.

Meg laughed at herself in the car mirror as she applied blusher to accent her high cheekbones, one of the tricks Blythe had taught her. She tucked her madras shirt into her white jeans.

"Tell me about your Aunt Harriet, Rick. What shall I call her? Mrs. . . . What is her last name?"

"Pearce. Miss. She's old—about eighty—and old-fashioned in the prim and proper mode. You'll be staying with her tonight."

"I'll call her Miss Pearce. Tell me more about her."

"Too late. We're here. Our land." The sweep of his arm encompassed dense woods close to the road with neat rows of plants on the hillside beyond. "Piet lives in that ugly A-frame. I'll have to stay with him tonight—so as not to offend Aunt Hat."

A short distance beyond the drive that led to the A-frame, Rick turned into another narrow lane bordered by vivid peonies, flowering trees, and low evergreens. To the left was a brown clapboard house.

"Lovely!" Meg clapped her hands together.

"Just the driveway, my dear. The entrance is around back." He parked in front of a three-car garage and checked his watch. "Not much time. I'll make the introductions and then retire to Piet's to put on my wedding garb."

He handed her the dress, picked up her tote, and led her through a low gate into a hedged garden—another riot of color—to a wide door with a bell hanging beside it.

He gave the clapper a tug and then opened the screen door and ushered Meg ahead of him into a narrow hall. Through a wide archway on the left she could see a low-ceilinged room with a fireplace and Dutch oven. Narrow stairs rose at one end of the room. "The original kitchen in the old farmhouse," Rick explained, "built in 1807."

"Here, Frederick." A strong voice called from the room opposite the front door.

Meg entered the room and stopped and stared. It was huge, a combination greenhouse, porch, living room, and library. "Oh, oh my," she breathed. "What a . . . beautiful, delightful . . . It's—"

"Isn't it? And you must be the hotshot lawyer Frederick has been telling me about."

"Fortunately, she is usually more articulate."

Rick laughed. "You—and your house—have overwhelmed her, Aunt Hat."

"And your peonies and all the plants in this room." Meg turned to focus on the woman sitting in a straight-backed chair in front of an old-fashioned rolltop desk. Meg had imagined a pretty little woman in the Helen Hayes manner; Harriet Pearce had square jaws and a square body. She looked Meg squarely in the eyes. Her mannishly cut hair was gray with streaks of black. She was wearing a no-style blue dress and old-lady tie shoes.

Rick stepped forward and kissed the woman's cheek.

Meg approached her with hand outstretched. "How do you do, Miss Pearce."

"I do fine." She shook Meg's hand firmly and turned to Rick. "I know you better than to think you plan to go to the wedding in a polo shirt, so get a move on or we'll be late. Piet's already at the church. He's ushering."

"Piet's an usher? Piet?" Rick set Meg's tote on the floor and hurried to the door.

"When's the last time you saw Jerry?" Miss Pearce called after him. "Five, six years ago? Piet and Jerry are pals." She turned to Meg. "Go don your finery, girl. Upstairs, first room on the right. Need anything, just look for it."

"Thank you, Miss Pearce. Rick and I appreciate—"

Miss Pearce dismissed her with a flick of her hand.

Twenty minutes later Meg was shaking her head at her reflection in the long mirror. The dress Rick had asked her to wear was totally inappropriate for a church wedding and a fried-chicken reception. Blythe had called it an "amusing little nothing" when she had brought it home to Meg. The tube of green silk hung from wide shoulder straps and yet clung to her waist and hips, like an expensive slip.

It had been perfect the only other time she had worn it, to a cocktail party at the Tavern on the Green. She smiled into the mirror as she remembered that party, which had honored a retiring vice president of Rick's agency. Until that evening, Meg had thought of herself as socially gawky. But not that night, in the company of the most attractive man in the room. Rick had kept her close by his side and introduced her to officers and account executives as if she were a rare and lovely flower. After the party, cuddled close in a horse-drawn carriage, he had proposed.

The dress was her favorite but it was all wrong today. She took a large paisley scarf from her tote and arranged it to cover her back and shoulders.

Hearing the crunch of Rick's car on gravel, she slipped her feet into green sandals and ran downstairs. Miss Pearce was waiting just outside the door, leaning heavily on a sturdy cane. Without comment she gripped Meg's arm with her other hand and they made their way slowly to the parking area in front of the garage.

The church looked like a photograph from a calendar entitled "Scenes of New England," white clapboard, perfectly symmetrical, simple spire, graveyard in the rear. While Rick drove off to search for a parking place, Meg helped Miss Pearce up the walk and the few steps to the church vestibule. The old lady nodded to almost every person who passed them. She said "hello" to some, and "well" to those who asked how she was. She shook hands with few and introduced Meg to none.

At last Rick came running toward the church and Meg noticed that he had chosen his tie and silk handkerchief to match her dress. The green looked just right with his navy blue blazer and white slacks. "Gorgeous, isn't he?" she whispered to Miss Pearce, who looked up at Meg, raised one eyebrow, and nodded.

"Piet, old boy!" Rick took the steps two at a time. Meg turned to face her future brother-in-law while Rick slapped him on the back with one hand and drew Meg close with the other. "Meet my beloved Meg."

Piet took her hand in both of his—his hands were huge—and they silently studied one another. He was blond like his brother but he was several inches taller and broader. His skin was weathered and his features less fine. Piet was pottery; Rick, porcelain. His too-obviously-rented, white dinner jacket pulled across his broad shoulders and flapped loosely around his hips. She held her breath while he scanned her features.

A smile slowly spread across his face and he turned to Rick. "Congratulations, brother."

Meg exhaled and relaxed. *Silly*, she said to herself. *Does it matter if he likes me? No. But it will be nice if he does.*

Piet escorted Miss Pearce down the aisle. Rick

and Meg followed. As the service began he took her hand and held it tightly. When the groom said "I do," he squeezed her hand. When the bride said "I do," she squeezed his. It was a promise. *I love you, Frederick de Graaf,* she said silently. *I will love you until death do us part.*

As they were leaving the church, Meg heard a woman squeal, "I told you it was Heartthrob." A couple who looked like Jack Sprat and his wife headed toward them grinning broadly. "Good to see you, Freddy Graaf," the man said, shaking Rick's hand.

"It's good to see you," he said and introduced Meg to two old school friends.

"I called him Heartthrob," the woman explained, "because that's what we called him when we were in high school. Piet was Dreamboat. Every girl panted after one or both of them. Piet dated several girls steadily from time to time but I don't believe Freddy ever dated any of us more than twice."

"I was waiting for this lovely lady," Rick said.

They chatted for a moment while Meg smiled without hearing. *Freddy Graaf!* That's what these old friends had called her handsome, distinguished fiancé, Frederick *de* Graaf. She laughed, trying to picture him as a grubby little boy. Grubby? Awkward? Pimply? Not Rick!

"I'm going to run Miss Pearce home. You can find Jerry and Laura's house okay?" Piet asked his brother.

Rick turned to the old lady. "Aren't you going to the reception, Aunt Hat?"

"No. Loud music. Rather have a sandwich. . . ."

Rick kissed her cheek. "Aunt Hat is Stonefield's aristocracy. She can do whatever she wants, can't you, darling?"

She didn't answer but turned and hobbled down the walk, supported by Piet.

"I like your town," Meg said as she and Rick walked along the main street toward the car. "But you misrepresented it. I was expecting a backwoods sort of place, not a neat little town with an art gallery and an open-air restaurant." She stopped to look into the window of the gallery where an arresting watercolor stood behind several pieces of pottery.

"That's new since I lived here. I understand that there are efforts to make Stonefield into a picture-postcard sort of place, like Stockbridge. Doubt it's possible."

The car felt like the inside of an oven and it hadn't cooled when they turned off the main highway onto a dirt lane and parked in a mowed pasture.

"Why don't you leave the scarf in the car?" Rick suggested.

"You don't think this dress is a little skimpy?"

"It's sophisticated, stunning. It puts emerald flecks in your hazel eyes. Positively alluring." He kissed her nose and then untied the scarf, folded it neatly, and put it in the glove compartment before he stepped around the car to hold the door.

"Wait," Piet called as he waved to them from the open window of an old black Mercedes. He was no longer wearing the dinner jacket. When he got out of the car, Meg saw why it had fit poorly. His shoulders were so incredibly broad that the shoulder seams on his plain white dress shirt were at least an inch above the edge of his shoulders. In order to stretch across his shoulders, the rented jacket had had to be many sizes too large for his torso and hips. *He's what they call a hunk,* Meg thought.

"How come you're driving that?" Rick asked, pointing to the Mercedes.

Piet shrugged. "Miss Pearce doesn't drive anymore and she can't climb up to my pickup."

"You're her chauffeur?"

"I guess you could say that. Come, I want to show you your wedding gift." Piet took each of them by the elbow and escorted them up the lane.

"Do you think you should get yourself a chauffeur's cap?" Rick's grin took the acid out of his question.

Piet didn't answer; perhaps he hadn't heard.

Ahead was a little yellow house and an attached carport. Round tables and chairs had been set up on the broad green lawn but the guests were all gathered together around the drinks table. The air was filled with taped music.

"One day Jerry and Laura will build a larger house on the knoll back there," Piet said. "Then they'll sell this. They call it the cracker box."

"It doesn't look like a box to me." Meg stopped to study the house. "Not with that old-fashioned dooryard garden. And that tree. . . . How did you find a tree that would bloom on command?"

"Not easily. It's a late-blooming crab apple, container grown. That's your gift, Fred."

"But I sent you a check for a hundred dollars."

"It cost a hundred dollars, wholesale."

"A hundred dollars for one tree?" Rick frowned.

"It's perfect," Meg said quickly. "It will bloom on their anniversaries and they'll think of you, Rick."

"The foliage will shade the door in the summer. In the fall the tree will be covered with marble-sized red apples—if the birds and the squirrels don't steal them." Piet led them into the garden. "Miss Pearce gave the perennials that are blooming now—the pinks and the columbine—and some that will bloom later in the summer. I gave the evergreens."

"And the planning and planting," Meg added. She squatted down and pulled a clump of grass from the pine-bark mulch surrounding the tree.

"What *are* you doing?" Rick took the grass from her hand and dropped it. Looking at her smudged fingers, she felt like a child who had been caught with her hand in the cookie jar. Piet grinned and handed her a tissue. Suddenly Rick grinned, too. "A tree! Thanks, Piet. The garden adds a lot to the house. I'm sure Jerry and Laura like it."

"Indeed we do." The bride and groom entered the garden. When the introductions and kissing were over, Jerry thanked Rick for the tree.

"I just love it, and you," Laura bubbled. "We're really glad you came home for our wedding, Freddy." She turned to smile at Meg. "We're glad you're here, too."

"So am I." Meg took Rick's hand. The newlyweds went off to welcome other guests. "I like your friends," Meg said to both brothers. "I'll bet she is the nurse every patient hopes to see come through the door. Pretty and friendly."

As the three of them headed toward the drinks

table, hands reached out to shake Rick's hand. *They love him in Stonefield,* Meg thought.

"Hey, one and all," Rick shouted. " 'Who is this beautiful woman?' That's what you are asking one another. I'll tell you. She is my fiancée, Meg Bower. She's from Vermont originally but she lived in Massachusetts while she went to Smith and Harvard Law. Now she's a lawyer with Savage, Smith, and Spencer . . ."

For a moment, Meg wished she could hide her hot face with her hands while she willed Rick to stop. His friends might be impressed by Smith and Harvard but none of them had ever heard of the three S's. Suddenly, she relaxed and smiled. Rick, loving Rick, was proud of her!

". . . I won't try to tell you the names of all my good friends here," Rick concluded, turning to her. "I'll just ask them to introduce themselves to you."

"And you?" one young woman called. "What are you doing these days, Freddy? Besides finding yourself a brilliant wife?"

"That's my most important achievement to date, but I also work with Jackson and Hawkins, the advertising agency that brings you some of your favorite commercials like 'Have a Haverford Beer' and 'Bigger and Better with Bishop's Brand.' "

He picked up a jug of wine, examined the label, set it down, and ushered Meg to the end of the table where he tapped the beer ball sitting in a washtub packed with ice.

"Guess you can afford to be picky about your wine," a balding man taunted. He was holding a baby while a toddler clung to his leg.

"Hi, Joe. What have you been doing, besides the obvious? How many kids in total?"

"Two others and I'm working for a builder during the week and rototilling gardens and clearing wood lots and doing whatever I can to make a buck. I work. Believe me I work." He turned away angrily.

"Poor Joe," Rick whispered to Meg. "He was one of the brightest guys in our class." He shook his head sadly.

"In your class?" Meg whispered. "He looks ten years older than you. At least."

"Blame it on the kids."

They ate at a table with some of Rick's friends. The food had been prepared by members of the bride's and groom's families. Meg laughed to herself as she compared the plate in front of her with the one that had been set before her at the victory celebration the previous evening. She had heaped this plate with fried chicken, deviled eggs, potato salad, three-bean salad, pickled beets, and fruit mold. The other had held two shrimp kabobs on wild rice surrounded by three crisp snow peas, two baby carrots, and a slice of tomato on a radicchio leaf.

Later, Piet stopped at their table and asked if he could get anyone anything from the buffet.

"Not for us." Rick sighed. "We're stuffed."

"Speak for yourself, Rick." Meg handed her plate to Piet. "I'd like another deviled egg and a small piece of chicken, a wing maybe?"

Piet's eyes twinkled as he nodded his approval of her appetite.

The best man toasted the bride and groom. The

cake was cut. Couples began to dance in the carport. Meg sat back and thought how much she liked Rick's town and his friends and his brother and his aunt. *I am one lucky woman,* she said to herself.

She wasn't hearing the conversation at the table until Piet shouted "Emily," and escorted a pretty woman with short strawberry-blond curls to their table. She was wearing a cotton caftan that announced rather than hid a pregnancy that was just beginning to show. "I want you to meet my brother, Fred, and his fiancée, Meg. Emily inherited the old Darrow place."

"That boarded-up, shingle—" Rick stopped short.

"Monstrosity." Emily laughed merrily. "Come see it now."

"Hear you've written a book about Myrna and William," one of the women at the table said.

"Are they still alive?" Rick asked, amazed. "Beavers," he explained to Meg.

"But growing old." Emily sighed. "They only had one kit this year. Keith thinks this may be their last summer."

"Keith is Dr. Cavanaugh, Emily's husband and a zoologist who has been studying the beavers," Piet explained. "He teaches at your alma mater, Rick."

"He's writing a scholarly book about beavers in North America," Emily said. "Together we've written a children's book about William and Myrna and their offspring. And the good news is that Natalie is going to illustrate it and we already have a publisher—thanks to her."

"Natalie's new since your time, Rick," Piet explained. "Bought the old Jackson place. She illustrates children's books."

A man with a beard came and stood behind Emily with his hands on her shoulders. When the congratulations on the book had died down, he whispered in her ear.

"I've worked all day at the gallery. Now my keeper here thinks I should go home and rest." She patted her little bulge. "So I'll say good night to all of you. It was nice to meet Piet's brother. Have Piet bring you by to see what he has done for our yard. It had been neglected so long . . . It was nice to meet you too, Meg."

Meg and Rick danced. When Piet cut in, Meg asked him to tell her more about Emily's beavers. "They must be named for Myrna Loy and William Powell. Could that be?"

"Right," he said. "Peter Darrow named them. He's the man who built the house." Piet looked at the dusky sky. "They swim out at about this time of night. Want to see them?"

"Oh yes. Please."

"We're going to visit the beavers," Piet called to his brother, who was dancing with the groom's mother. "Shall we wait for you?"

"I don't care about the beavers. Neither does Meg."

"Oh yes, I do. I certainly care about beavers named William and Myrna." She laughed and put her hand on Piet's arm and they strolled down the lane.

Across the road another lane led toward a brown shingle house with a veranda and a tower. "That's

Emily's house?" Meg asked. "And she inherited it? From her parents? Grandparents?"

"A stranger. Peter Darrow built the house for Emily's grandmother, a fickle lady who married someone else. You should see the inside. Octagonal living room. Stained-glass window on the landing to the stairway. I'll make arrangements to show it to you sometime, if you like."

"I'd like that very much."

Two dogs ran to greet them in the lane, barking loudly but at the same time wagging their tails.

"Quiet," Piet commanded. The dogs obeyed and followed along behind them when they turned toward an ugly pond filled with dead trees and mounds of sticks.

At the edge of the pond three young beavers were tumbling together. "The one-year-olds," Piet explained. "When they're two, their parents will kick them out to find or make their own ponds. Keith says that there isn't enough undeveloped land for them around here so he's been trapping the two-year-olds and taking them up into the Adirondacks."

"Kick them out? William and Myrna evict their own children? That's not—" She clipped the sentence short. Who was she to judge beaver behavior?

Piet studied her face until she turned away, embarrassed. "Don't worry about them, Meg. Two-year-old beavers are adults, ready to find mates for themselves."

The water in the pond was marked by two vees with a beaver head at the point of each. "Hey, Myrna and William," Piet called. "Meet my brother's fiancée, Meg Bower. She's come all the way from New York City to see you." The beavers did not acknowledge the introduction. "Forgive them," Piet said. "They're so famous here in Stonefield that they've become uppity. They seldom speak to the local people, let alone to strangers."

Meg giggled her appreciation of his whimsy. "They've been together for a long time?" she asked.

"Probably since they were two-year-olds. Beavers mate for life. I think that's one of the reasons Peter Darrow loved them so much, because they are faithful."

"Myrna and William are the first beavers I ever met," Meg whispered. "They're superior to many people, aren't they? Monogamous. And they care for their—" Her voice broke. She straightened her shoulders and finished the sentence. "Beavers care for their children until their children are ready to care for themselves. I'm very pleased to have made your acquaintance, William and Myrna. Very pleased, indeed." She turned back toward the lane.

Piet touched her hand and pointed to the rising moon and its shimmery path through the surface of the pond. They stood side by side in silence until Meg spoke. "It's enchanted. Thank you, Piet."

When they returned to the reception, they found Rick laughing with a group of men and women who must have been his classmates. He reached out for Meg. She snuggled close, welcoming the shelter of his body against the cooling night air.

Chapter Two

A warm breeze brushed her cheek, inviting Meg to open her eyes. She stretched and inched herself up on the feather pillow to look around at the calico print wallpaper, ruffled white curtains, and patchwork quilt. Although the room was awash in sunlight, it was only 6:30. She slid back down into the sheets and closed her eyes.

The birds were chirpy. Light penetrated her lids. She turned over and buried her head in the pillow —for a moment. Throwing back the sheet and quilt, she sat up and pivoted her body toward the window. When she was on her feet she stretched and yawned elaborately. And then she looked out of the window and stood motionless, in awe.

Below her, irregularly shaped islands of plants and flowers rose from a sea of lawn. Not the coveted "lawn like green velvet" but a grassy lawn dotted with spots of purple and changes in texture. Huge trees spread their arms to shade and shelter some of the islands. Meg reached for her white jeans without turning away from the window.

Minutes later she stepped through a wide screen door in the greenhouse/library where she leaned against the door frame and put on the sneakers she had carried down with her. And then she stepped out across the dew-studded lawn. One enormous maple tree shaded a peaceful garden filled with hostas and a plant with dark leaves below budding plumes. Dropping to her knees, she studied a group of exquisite three-inch-high pink daisylike flowers blooming a few inches above delicate foliage. "You're each a flawless jewel," she whispered. "I wish you'd tell me your name."

"Anemonella."

"A-nem-o-nella," Meg repeated as she turned her head to smile up at Piet. "Anemonella."

He lifted a thermos and an oversized mug from the wheelbarrow in front of him. "Hope you like your coffee black."

"I always drink it black and coffee will make an already perfect morning even better. What's better than perfect?"

"A sunny morning in June." He handed her the filled mug and pushed the wheelbarrow on across the lawn. He was whistling the obvious tune, "June is Bustin' Out All Over." Meg sang it under her breath as she walked up one grassy path and down another. From time to time she paused to sip her coffee and to admire the peonies and the columbines and dozens of plants she could not name. One of the flower gardens in full sun was bordered with lettuce and parsley. She broke off a piece of lettuce and ate it. Tomato plants grew among daisies. She sighed as she remembered another garden where lettuce and tomatoes had been crowded with weeds. She shook that garden out of her memory and concentrated on this new garden memory.

Rhododendrons and azaleas were massed in front of a high stone wall. She walked along the lawn beside them. When the wall and the shrubbery made a right angle, she turned to continue to follow it. There were occasional breaks in the greenery revealing windows with marble sills but no glass. Again the wall turned.

Before her was yet another miracle. She stood for a moment, staring in wonder. Then she spread her arms and ran down a ramp into an enclosed area many feet below the level of the lawns. "A secret garden!" she whispered, clasping her hands beneath her chin as she turned to gaze at the trees espaliered to the old walls and at the beds filled with flowers and vegetables.

Leaning forward from the seat of a golf cart, Miss Pearce was carefully pruning twigs from a miniature rose, one of many planted in a raised bed. She looked up at Meg and smiled. "Good morning. You may help Piet weed the tomatoes."

Rick's brother was on his knees in front of a large bed filled with vegetables. Green marble-sized tomatoes clung to the vines he was tying to poles.

"I saw blooms but no tomatoes on the plants up above," Meg exclaimed.

"She's observant," Miss Pearce said. "That's good."

"These walls hold the heat so that we can set out

the tomato plants here before the last frost elsewhere," Piet explained. "We put a panel of plastic above them to protect them on cold nights. Do you want to weed? You don't have to."

Her answer was to take a dandelion digger and a fork from the tool box. They worked in silence until Miss Pearce announced that she was hungry and drove her silent cart near them. She turned in her seat to a cooler sitting in the area designed to hold golf clubs. When she had arranged fruit, yogurt, and big bran muffins on a napkin, she invited Piet and Meg to help themselves.

"I suppose Fred is still sleeping," she said.

"You suppose wrong, Aunt Hat," Rick called as he ran down the ramp toward them. "We have a golf game scheduled for ten-thirty. Did you forget, Meg? Hurry and eat something and then go change." He kissed her cheek and helped himself to a container of yogurt.

Dismayed, she extended one leg, and pointed to the grass and dirt stains on the knee of her white jeans.

"So put on something else, Meg," Rick said.

"I have another shirt but these are the only pants I brought. Actually, I just haven't had time to tend to my laundry. These were my only clean pants; I meant to keep them clean but I forgot when I had this chance to—"

"Play in the dirt?" he asked, patting her head as if she were a two-year-old.

"I'd forgotten just how much I like to play in the dirt. I like mud even more." She laughed and then sobered quickly. "I can't go play golf today. I am sorry, Rick."

"So you'll have to stay home with us." Miss Pearce handed her a banana. "Gardening is better exercise than golf. Cancel your date, Frederick."

"The date is with C. Randolph Montgomery, vice president in charge of advertising of the Webster Corporation, and his daughter." Rick spoke through clenched teeth. "There is no way I can cancel."

"Go without me, Rick. Please." Meg took his arm in both of her hands and walked away from Miss Pearce and Piet. "You can wow the daughter and—" She stopped short. "Look at that circular wall. You never told me, Rick, that this place is magical. One delight after another. The peonies along the lane, the entry garden, that magnificent garden room. Yesterday I was struck dumb. And this morning I discovered so much more. Acres of lawns and plants. And finally, this! A secret garden. It's like a fairy tale."

He grinned at her. "Okay, darling. You play up to Aunt Hat and I'll go off and wow Miss Montgomery." He lifted her grimy hand and looked at it critically. "Don't get too carried away with this 'little farmer' role, Meg. One of the reasons I love you is that you are a sophisticated New Yorker." He kissed her lightly, slapped her bottom, and headed off toward the A-frame. "I'll probably have lunch at the club," he called back over his shoulder.

Meg returned to sit on a low wall near the golf cart while she finished her muffin. "Delicious," she said happily. "Now please tell me about this place. How did it come to be?"

"Very simple," the old lady said, chuckling. "All it took was money and hard work."

"And love," Meg added. "Someone once told me that all growing things need food, water, and love."

When she looked up at Piet for confirmation of her formula, he turned away abruptly and spoke with his back to them. "I'm going to see if there's any sign of life in that new holly and then I'll run into town to pick up your paper, Miss Pearce. Anything else while I'm there?"

"No, dear. But thank you." She reached out and patted his hand.

Why, Meg asked herself, *did Piet call this old woman Miss Pearce while Rick called her Aunt Hat?*

"I'll leave the paper by your chair." He turned to Meg. "Don't let her stay out here too long; she's not very smart when it comes to taking care of herself. I probably won't see you and Fred before you go back to the city. I'm glad to have met you, Meg. Fred's a lucky man." He turned and ran up the ramp.

Miss Pearce watched Piet until he disappeared, then she turned to Meg. "You want to hear about this place?"

"Please. I could pull the grass out of this bed while I listen. Okay?"

"Dig deeply to get the roots. It doesn't do any good to just chop off the tops." Miss Pearce settled back in her cart and told Meg about her socially ambitious great-grandfather who had bought the land and the farmhouse. He intended to build a shingle "summer cottage" in the style of the enormous cottages in Newport, Rhode Island, but his cottage burned to the ground before it was finished.

"Nothing was left standing but the cellar walls and the chimneys. The circular area was the foundation for the turret corner. After the fire, he more or less abandoned the place. So did my grandfather when he inherited it. Grandpa was a city banker who thought that any place more than twenty miles from Boston was wilderness."

Miss Pearce said that her grandfather and her mother died in the influenza epidemic of 1918, soon after her father had returned from France. "Papa and I—I was eight—came here. Stop!" She glared at Meg. "Those leaves are feeding the daffodil bulbs. Don't touch them."

"I'm sorry. I just thought they looked so droopy. I didn't know."

Miss Pearce shrugged her acceptance of Meg's apology. "I can still remember how it looked when we first arrived. The farmhouse was so filthy that we had to stay in a boarding house for several weeks while it was being cleaned and painted. This was a mass of charred timbers and broken glass. It was horrible. As soon as the farmhouse was livable—the garden room came much later—Papa had a crew in to clean out this place. They carted away truckloads of debris. Papa planned to have the cellar filled with dirt, but one magic evening after supper he and I walked out here and we climbed down into the cellar and I said, 'Look, Papa, it's just like Mary Lenox's secret garden.' He didn't know what I was talking about but before I went to bed I gave him my copy of *The Secret Garden*, the book by Frances Hodgson Burnett, you know. The next morning he said, 'Would you like a secret garden, Hattie?' The old lady smiled beatifically.

"You've lived here all of your life?"

"No."

Meg waited for her to say more but Miss Pearce remained mute while she put the food back in the cooler and drove the cart back to her miniature rose bed. The two women worked in silence until Meg remembered Piet's instructions and reminded the old lady that they had been at it quite a long time.

"I'm not tired." She looked at Meg's stained jeans. "But I expect you'd like to launder those jeans before Frederick gets back. You can do your sheets at the same time and any whites in the hamper."

While her clothes were in the washer, Meg bathed in the huge tub on legs and then sat on the lawn in her robe and read the *Times* Piet had delivered. When the clothes had been moved to the dryer, she and Miss Pearce worked the puzzle together. It was three-thirty when Meg heard a car stop in front of the garage. She ran to dress before Rick could see her in dishabille.

When she returned to the lawn in her sparkling jeans, she saw that he was sitting on the edge of a chair facing Miss Pearce.

"She's lovely, and has the makings of a fine gardener," Miss Pearce said, laughing.

"She's already a fine lawyer." Rick sighed. "I just wish we could get married."

"Why don't you?"

"Because we have no place to live. Have you any

idea of Manhattan rents? A studio at a thousand a month is a bargain."

"So move to Queens or Brooklyn or the suburbs."

"Brooklyn Heights is almost as expensive as Manhattan. No, the only thing to do is to buy a cooperative apartment. Something small in a good neighborhood. For about two hundred fifty thousand dollars we could get three rooms on the Upper East Side."

"If you had a quarter of a million, which I assume you do not."

"No, but if we had a down payment. . . ." He shook his head sadly.

Could he be begging Miss Pearce for money? Meg was aghast; years ago she had promised herself never to beg anyone for anything again. "How was the golf game?" she asked, forcing a smile.

"Productive, I think."

"You win?" Miss Pearce asked.

"That wasn't the point, Aunt Hat."

"What *is* the point of playing a game, if it's not to win?"

"Contacts, in this case." He rose to his feet. "Best we be on our way. Traffic will be fierce."

Meg took the old lady's hand. This time her smile was genuine. "Thank you, Miss Pearce. I loved being here. Thank you for the bed, the food, and for letting me play in the dirt. I'd forgotten how much I like that."

"Gardening is good for you, girl. Anytime you want to come dig in the soil, just give me a call. I can use all the help I can get." Rick and Meg were almost to the parking area when the old lady called after them. "I meant that, Meg. I'd be glad to have you come for a visit—anytime."

When they were on the narrow road leading to the highway, Meg hugged herself and sighed. "What a wonderful weekend, Rick. Thank you." She kissed his cheek and then asked about the golf game again, and about the Montgomery father and daughter. "Are they good golfers?"

"Very good. Jocelyn is not as good as her father but she is better than I. But that's okay. I didn't slow the game and I managed to get in a few licks for my agency."

"Is Jocelyn pretty?"

"She's attractive. She teaches at one of the private schools in the city. I didn't catch which one. She's something of a social butterfly, I guess. Benefit balls. That kind of thing. Old money. Speaking of old money, you really made a hit with Aunt Hat."

"*She* made a hit with me, but you should have prepared me, Rick. I all but jumped out of my skin when she shouted at me as I was about to cut the tops off daffodils." Meg laughed. "And then she told me to wash my own sheets, and hers too, as it turned out. Does she live there all alone, Rick?"

"Piet's hooked up a buzzer so that she can signal him anytime, and she has daily help, inside and out. You don't have to worry about Aunt Hat except to figure out how we can get her to part with a down payment on an apartment."

Meg studied Rick's profile. "Are you serious, Rick?" she asked at last.

"Of course I'm serious. I want to live with you."

His voice was so wistful that Meg had to swallow before she could speak. "We could live in the suburbs. It would probably be cheaper and we could have a little garden. . . ."

"You'd live in the boonies and spend hours every day on the train? Maybe someday we can have an apartment with a balcony or a terrace. Or a penthouse! Would you like a penthouse—when you're a partner and I'm a vice president? Step one is a 'beginner' apartment."

"On Fifth Avenue! You're a dreamer, Rick."

"Actually, I'd never considered Fifth Avenue before, but I doubt that we can get an apartment for less than two hundred and fifty anyplace unless the maintenance fee is over a thousand. So, my dear, you just keep smiling at Aunt Hat . . ."

"How come Piet calls her Miss Pearce? I take it she's not really your aunt. So why did she educate you?"

"Because I'm a charming fellow." Rick laughed. "She would have sent Piet to school too, anyplace he chose—and could get into. The old dear has no children, not even nieces or nephews. I don't know why Piet still calls her Miss Pearce; I call her aunt because she likes it."

"She likes you too, but maybe she thinks that a fine—and very expensive—education is enough. Room, board, and tuition at Williams, and then an apartment and living expenses and tuition at Columbia." Meg added numbers in her head. "She had to have spent more than a hundred thousand dollars by the time you got your MBA."

"I know I've been lucky." He reached over and patted her hand, including her in his good luck.

They drove with only the radio to break the silence for most of a half hour. Suddenly Rick spoke. "Why don't you ever tell me about your childhood or your parents, Meg? Why didn't someone help you through school?"

"They did. Strangers helped with a raft of scholarships and aid packages."

"So what about your family?"

"They had no money."

"Is that all you're going to tell me?" he asked.

"I think so." She lowered her voice to a seductive whisper. "I want to be a mystery woman. Doesn't that excite you?" She put her hand on his thigh.

"You excite me, all right. You'd excite me if you were not a mystery."

"So you tell me about your family."

"I told you that my father came here from Holland soon after the war, and that he was a landscape architect. In the late fifties he went back to Holland and married my mother—she was much younger than he. She was never happy here and she went home to live with her sister the same year that I went away to college. Dad spent several months every winter with her in Holland. He died in eighty-seven and Mother is remarried and living in Rotterdam."

"So's mine."

"Your mother is living in Rotterdam?"

"No. She's remarried. He's dead."

Rick sighed. "I assume that the 'he' is your father, not the man your mother married. Is there a reason why you use pronouns instead of their names? Is your mother's name She?" He laughed for a moment and then sobered into another awkward silence.

At last Meg spoke. "Look, Rick, I just don't get all nostalgic about my childhood. He was a nice man, an engineer who became a hippie farmer. She walked out when I was seven." Meg's voice broke.

Rick stroked her cheek and began to talk about a new ad campaign. One of the things Meg appreciated about Rick was his ability to fill awkward silences with amusing chatter.

"You hungry?" he asked as they neared the city.

"I hadn't thought about it but, yes, I am hungry. You? You ate after your game?"

"I never eat much when I'm working. Which reminds me that I've got to write a clever letter to Montgomery. One that sounds completely spontaneous. They're the hardest."

"And I have to read a packet of papers that Mr. Spencer handed me just before the party Friday night."

"So let's turn in the car and then go to Dino's for a quick beer and hamburger and then to your place or mine. I'll write a draft of my letter while you read whatever you have to read. Have it with you? It would be so much easier if we were married."

"We'd have our dinners all lined up in the freezer. Wouldn't take a minute to pop them into the microwave."

"After we'd made our selections," Rick added.

They laughed together, each knowing that the other was remembering the night early last autumn when they had met in front of the frozen dinner section at D'Agostino's. He'd stood studying the selection while she'd reached around him to load her cart.

"Good?" he'd asked, as she'd pulled a chicken dinner from the case.

"No," she'd answered honestly. "Unless you have a taste for salty cardboard."

"So why are you buying it?"

"I don't know." She'd put it back and selected three other dinners. "These are actually not too bad. The truth is that I think in terms of quick and cheap. I wouldn't be here now except that I scraped the peanut butter jar clean last night."

"I understand perfectly." He'd put three of the dinners she'd suggested in his cart. "I work long hours. Advertising. How about you?"

"Law," she'd said, really looking at him for the first time. His blond hair had been mussed, a pleasant note of incongruity against his crisp striped shirt, pressed suit, and polished loafers. Their eyes had met and she remembered being glad that she was wearing a new silk blouse. He had told her later that he had admired her slim hands and tapered fingers before he had even looked at the rest of her.

"So," he had said very slowly, as if weighing the pros and cons of an important issue, "why don't we just put these boxes back in the freezer and go down the street for a quick dinner made by some-one else?"

She had hesitated. She'd never in her life been anyone's pickup. But he was so attractive. "I have a lot of work tonight . . ."

He'd lifted his briefcase to indicate that he was

bringing work home, too. "We'll make it fast and then we'll come back here to stock our freezers."

She had nodded and their fast dinner had taken almost three hours. It would have taken longer except that they were both dedicated to their work. That was something they shared, respect for one another's time. They talked nightly on the phone. They usually met once during the week for a quick dinner together. They spent at least part of every weekend together. They were perfect for one another—smart and ambitious.

She placed her hand on the back of his neck. "This has been a lovely weekend," she whispered.

"It's not over yet." He raised an eyebrow and his suggestive smile made Meg feel deliciously sexy.

It was almost nine o'clock before they were seated on the carpet in his room with their backs against his bed, she with the papers she had to study, he with a lined pad on which he would write the first draft of his "casual" note.

Two hours later she had read three pages; he had written "Dear Mr. Montgomery—and Jocelyn" on his lined pad. *Working* together was not possible—not tonight. They agreed on that and he walked her home where she had every intention of poring over her papers for several hours. He kissed her again at her door. The girls in his high school class had called him Heartthrob. She understood that completely.

Chapter Three

INSTEAD of studying her papers, Meg fell asleep soon after midnight. Monday morning she woke slowly and late from a wispy dream in which two blond men strolled in and out of a garden. Later, during a meeting with other associates and Mr. Spencer, the partner who headed the mergers and acquisitions division, her thoughts returned to the garden and Stonefield and the beavers. She and Rick would be as constant as the beavers.

"Do you foresee any problems here, Meg?" Mr. Spencer asked.

Meg stared at him blankly. "I'm sorry," she whispered.

"You did have a chance to look through the papers I gave you Friday?"

She nodded. "I . . . ah . . ."

"We have a situation here that requires our full attention, Meg."

"Of course, Mr. Spencer. I apologize." Meg felt blood rush to her face. It was the first time in the more than two years she had been with the firm that she had been chastised publicly. "It won't happen again."

She meant that! Meg had devoted the last ten years of her life to being "the best." The few B's that had ruined her straight A average at Smith had pained her. She had been in the top ten percent of her Harvard Law School class. She was one of the best-paid third-year law associates in the country.

Mr. Spencer dismissed her with a nod. Another associate continued the discussion of problems facing the client, Dixon. The international company produced a variety of engines. Recently, a trio of young mavericks had started a company they called Smengines to manufacture small engines and parts for small engines. Their products were priced so cheaply that they threatened Dixon's small-engine division. The large company was now preparing for a hostile takeover of the smaller one. Meg concentrated on the details of the case, shoving all thoughts of gardens and blond brothers out of her mind.

When she returned to her office, she asked herself why Dixon didn't look for a way to meet the competition's lower prices? It seemed to Meg that the client was wrong—a heretical thought; the client is never wrong. Dixon would buy out Smengines and raise prices to cover the buy-out price and the legal fees. *Who cares?* she asked herself. The answer to the question was obvious. *I care. It's my job to care.*

Meg worked straight through the lunch hour and on until six o'clock when she could not sit at her desk one more minute. She loaded her briefcase with all of the papers she still had to study before her meeting with Mr. Spencer the following morning. Passing the open door of the office next to hers she called out a defiant "good night."

Joel, an intense, owlish young man who had been first in his class at Chicago Law, looked up through wire-rimmed glasses. "You're leaving? Already?"

Meg pointed to her stuffed briefcase and continued a few steps down the hall where she stopped and turned back to enter his office. "Joel," she said, waiting until he again raised his eyes from the papers spread out in front of him. "I want to ask you a personal question—which you are perfectly free not to answer. Don't you ever resent the hours we spend doing work that is often boring?"

"Boring?" He scratched his head as if he couldn't believe what he was hearing.

"Boring. Not always but sometimes." Against her better judgment, she plunged on. "Don't you realize that most people in New York are already home? They have put in their seven or eight hours and they're having a drink or bathing the kids or watching the news on television. They'll be eating soon and then maybe they'll go to the movies or for a walk. They can go to bed early and read. Do you know that people out there actually have time to read novels? When's the last time you read anything just for the fun of it? Even an article in the *Times*? Yesterday I actually wasted an hour on the Sunday puzzle. I haven't done that for two years. It was fun."

He grinned. "You sound like my wife, and I say

to you what I say to her: the prize is worth the struggle."

"Are you talking about the money?" Meg asked, knowing that she and he were already making more than 99.9 percent of the people in New York their age.

"The money, and the prestige and the position. The chance to work with other bright people. The challenge. The variety of cases. I love my work. You do too, Meg. You're just out of sorts today." He picked up a paper on his desk and began to read it.

"You're probably right. Thanks for letting me blow off steam, but Joel, don't concentrate so much on the future that you neglect the now."

He looked up again and grinned. "Okay, Meg. I'll try to get home before nine. My wife will thank you, but just to set the record straight, I always spend Saturday evening and all day Sunday with her. Sometimes we do the puzzle."

She saluted him and went on down the hall to the reception room, where she saluted the dead partners hanging in ornate gilt frames over glass-doored cases of leather-bound law books. When Meg had entered this room for the first time, she had known immediately that this old, respected firm was the firm for her.

And today I came to a meeting unprepared. Meg was still chagrined, but she went on down the elevator feeling more at ease than she had felt at any time since the morning meeting. Her sense of well-being lasted all the way down to the lobby and across to the revolving doors.

Stepping out onto Madison Avenue, she was

struck by a blast of air so hot that she almost retreated. Instead she turned right and walked uptown, looking back to see if a bus was coming. When, several minutes later, a bus passed her she did not run to catch it at the stop ahead. It was crowded and the thought of rubbing sweaty shoulders with strangers was odious. She considered walking over to Lexington Avenue to catch a subway. To enter a crowded air-conditioned car, however, she might have to wait who knew how many minutes in the ovenlike station. She resisted the idea of hailing a cab, choosing instead to walk to Third Avenue where she could also catch an uptown bus. It was too hot to walk all of the way home—and it would take too long.

She walked along thinking of nothing except the heat until she was assaulted by an odor so fetid she pinched her nostrils together with her fingers. Garbage spilled from plastic bags near the back door of a fancy restaurant. In another block she almost stepped in a plop of dog feces and she began to notice other dog odors. She smiled wryly to herself. She loved dogs and often went out of her way to pass a pet store. If only someone would enforce the city's pooper-scooper laws, especially in the summer.

On Lexington Avenue her senses were assaulted again by a tall young man, unshaven and dirty, who stepped directly in front of her and asked for a dollar. She stepped to the right; he stepped with her. She stepped to the left; he did, too.

"I give money to the soup kitchen at Saint Mark's. If you need anything, go there." Other pedestrians, hearing the anger in her voice, stopped to listen. The bum shrugged and turned away.

When she could dismiss the encounter from her mind, she was surprised to see that she was only ten blocks from her apartment. The soles of her feet burned and her cotton dress clung to her back. Her neck was damp and her hair lay plastered against her cheek. She was, in short, miserable, but she plodded on.

Just around the corner from her building she was greeted by a familiar "Hel-lo mis-sy" from her favorite Korean greengrocer. He pointed to a stack of beautiful tomatoes. "Tas-ty," he said. She left his little shop with three tomatoes, a cucumber, and red-leaf lettuce.

She had showered and eaten a sandwich and salad, and was lying across her bed in her air-conditioned room, studying the case and sipping iced tea, when Rick called. Unfortunately for him, he asked about her day.

"On a scale of one to ten, it was minus twenty." She told him about being unprepared at the meeting and about her walk home. "Some days I hate the legal racket and other days I hate living in New York City and today I hated both. So how was your day?"

His day had been terrific, he said. "Don't let the weather warp your perspective, Meg. You love your work and New York is the most exciting city in the world. I took cabs today and breathed nothing but cooled air, except for the few seconds it took to get from doorways to curbs. I wish I could convince you to take cabs, Meg."

"Once I've paid off my loans, I'll take cabs everywhere—unless I hire my own car and driver." She laughed. "You know why I love you, Rick? You restore my good humor. I loved being in Stonefield. I wish we were going back next weekend."

"But we'll enjoy the great out-of-doors at the partners' pool party on Long Island. That will be fun."

Meg grimaced. She hated business gatherings that were *supposed* to be fun; she couldn't imagine they ever were.

The partners' pool party was always held on the last Sunday in June on the Long Island estate of the senior partner, Archibald Savage. Long ago, when wives promoted their husband's careers rather than pursuing careers of their own, the partners' wives and their cooks had actually prepared the food. The firm had been smaller then. This year the extravagant feast for the ninety-five associates was prepared by a caterer and paid for out of the thirty-two partners' profits.

In previous years, Meg had come out on the train with other first- and second-year associates. She had felt self-conscious in her bathing suit and ill at ease as she mingled with senior associates and partners. The hours of forced frivolity had seemed endless. The only pleasant moments she could remember were those during which she had walked alone through the formal rose garden.

This year was entirely different because Rick was with her. He drove her in a rented sports car. When little Mr. Smith, who had been coxswain on his college crew, began to describe every event in a championship season, Rick not only listened, he asked questions and laughed appreciatively when the man described being thrown into the filthy Thames after a Henley Regatta. He listened to another partner's description of his Buddha collection. He swam with Meg in the pool and told her that she was gorgeous in her black tank suit.

A first-year associate confirmed what Rick said when she and Meg met in the cabana. "Listen to this, Meg. I just overheard Hennesey say to Spencer, 'Take a look at young Bower. What a figure. Think we could send her into a courtroom in a bathing suit?' And Spencer said, 'She's smart, too. In fact, she has everything going for her. She's engaged to that handsome blond on the diving board.' That's a verbatim report, Meg. Your Rick doesn't by any chance have a brother, does he?"

"He does and he looks like Rick, but he's taller, broader, and older." Meg laughed. "And he lives in Massachusetts."

"Have degree, will travel." The young associate ran out and jumped into the pool feet first.

Meg brushed her hair smooth, put on a black eyelet cover-up and went out to sit beside the pool with Rick. This business party *was* fun. She looked at Joel and his wife standing alone under an enormous beech tree, looking uncomfortable. She picked up the *Times* magazine section from the slates beside her chaise and waved it at them. They understood immediately and drew up chairs so that the four of them could speed through the puzzle in a record twenty minutes.

Later, when they had heaped their plates at the buffet, Meg and Rick were invited to sit at a table for twelve with Mrs. Savage, another partner and his wife, and five other associates, and two spouses.

"Hear you're working on the Smengines takeover, Meg," a first-year associate said from across the table.

Shocked, she leaned toward him with a hand on either side of her mouth to form a screen. *Shut up,* she mouthed. He knew better than to discuss a client's business in front of four outsiders—five, counting Mrs. Savage. "How about some more wine?" she said, lifting the bottle from the coaster, even though the partner had just filled everyone's glasses. He smiled wryly at Meg, took a big gulp of his wine, and held his glass for a refill.

"I don't un—" one of the wives started to say before she received a signal, most likely a kick, from her husband.

"I've never been in this area of Long Island before," Rick said smoothly. "We passed a number of fine old estates. I assume it's a long-established community, Mrs. Savage. Eighteenth century?"

It was the ideal question. Mrs. Savage, an officer in the local historical society, beamed at Rick. She spoke, with humor and affection, about the eighteenth-century buildings in her own and surrounding towns.

Bless you, Rick. Meg reached over and squeezed the hand in his lap. He had such a talent for saying the right thing at the right time!

Word of the associate's faux pas spread. Soon after they had finished eating, Mr. Savage took Meg and Rick to one side. He told Meg that he had heard from the partner at her table that she had handled a difficult situation well. He thanked Rick for jumping into the silence. "There's nothing my wife would rather talk about than local history. I can't imagine how you knew that."

Rick didn't mention the episode until they were on the Long Island Expressway heading back to the city. "So explain what was going on while we were having dinner, Meg. All the guy said was something about you working on the Smengines takeover. Could any company actually have such a silly name? Or is it silly? I remembered it. Smengines. Must be a contraction of 'small engines.' If you are in the market for a small engine you'll think Smengines. So it's not a silly name; it's clever." He nodded, agreeing with himself. "So what was going on at the table? You'd have thought that the poor guy had announced that the emperor had no clothes."

"You were wonderful, Rick. Just wonderful. I really enjoyed this party; last year I hated it. The difference was that you were with me."

He kissed his finger and laid it on her cheek. "I could see you were upset. Smengines is your client?"

"No, but any information about a client's business is sacred. We're like priests in the confessional. You must erase what the associate said from your mind. Never repeat it. Don't even think of it."

"Say no more, lovely lady. My lips are sealed." He grinned at her and then concentrated on the congested highway. Everyone and his relatives appeared to be returning from one of the Long Island beaches to the city.

Chapter Four

THE next day, Rick broke one of their sacred rules and phoned her at work. "You've got to get away by six o'clock this evening, Meg. The fellow I told you about who is buying the apartment on Fifth Avenue has invited us to come see it. I accepted for both of us."

"But Rick, I don't give a tinker's—"

"I do, Meg. Please. Just look at it. That's all I ask."

She laughed at his intensity and agreed to meet him there.

The doorman eyed her suspiciously and held the door open a mere crack while she gave the name of Rick's friend and the apartment number. Then he allowed her to enter a small vestibule where he phoned upstairs. At last he held the lobby door and motioned her toward the elevator. As she passed a large mirror she looked at herself carefully. Did she really look like a thief or a . . . ? What else could the doorman fear? A kidnapper? A terrorist with a bomb? Her dress was a little wrinkled. She smoothed it as best she could. Her navy blue pumps were well polished. It must have been the brown briefcase. Perhaps she should have had a color-coordinated briefcase—or no briefcase—to enter such an august establishment.

Rick had arrived before her. His friend, a balding man in his early forties, led them through the long narrow foyer to the long narrow living room. Standing in front of one of the two windows, she looked down into a cement courtyard and across to a brick wall. Meg, who was well acquainted with dismal housing, rated this room as super dismal. Nothing could grow in these windows, not even sword plants or philodendron.

"I'll have to do something about the windows," the owner said. "What do you think, Meg? Vertical blinds?" Fortunately, he didn't wait for an answer. "And I'll have to build a closet at the end of the foyer to make room for the boys' futons and junk. They live with their mother but she likes to have me take them off her hands as many weekends as possible." He led her into the dark bedroom with a single window which also opened onto the brick wall, past the bathroom and through the small kitchen. "So what do you think?" he asked.

"It's terrific, isn't it?" Rick said.

Meg looked from one of them to the other. *Terrific?* She couldn't imagine anyone but bats mustering enthusiasm for this cave. "I like the moldings," she said.

She was relieved when the phone rang and she heard Rick's friend say, "Send her up." He turned back to them to announce that the painting contractor had arrived. "What colors would you choose, Meg?"

"White," she said decisively as she took Rick's arm. "Thanks for showing us your new home. We hope you'll be very happy . . ."

He nodded and opened the door to the hall. Rick enthused for a few more minutes. They left when the elevator door opened and a young woman with a clipboard got out.

Rick's eyes were aglow with excitement when he turned to her on the sidewalk in front of the building and then motioned across the street. "Just think how you'd love stepping out of your doorway to look at Central Park every morning, Meg. Isn't that great? Such a dignified old building."

"Such a dignified old monster for a doorman, and such small, dark rooms."

"But Central Park is right across the street."

"True, but how much time would you spend standing on the sidewalk looking at it? The windows of the apartment, you may have noticed, have a simply fascinating view of a brick wall."

"How about an apartment in the front of the building, overlooking the park? Would you like that, darling?" His voice was *too* sweet.

She shrugged her shoulders and took his arm. "Sure," she said, laughing. "As long as we're dreaming we might just as well dream big. How about a view of Central Park and at least one more room to use as a study and an extra bathroom, and a kitchen with a dishwasher, and solid gold doorknobs and huge closets and . . ." She turned serious. "I feel sorry for his boys. It would have been nice if they could have had their own space in their father's apartment."

Meg had supposed they would have dinner together, but as they approached a subway entrance, Rick announced that he had an appointment. He didn't say where or with whom. He just kissed her on the cheek and disappeared down the station stairs.

Meg walked on toward home, bewildered. Was Rick mad at her because she didn't take the apartment seriously? Could he honestly even consider living in a high-priced hole just because it was on Fifth Avenue? *Forget it,* she said to herself. *We can't afford it—fortunately.*

Meg let herself into her own lobby with her own key. The apartment Blythe had divided into two bed-sitters was about the same size as the one she had just visited. The bath and the kitchen were off a square foyer. Blythe occupied the living room. The bedroom was Meg's.

Before going into her room, Meg took a dinner from the freezer and popped it into the microwave. The window in Meg's room overlooked the roofs of brownstones in the next block and the towers of the midtown skyline. She could not grow flowers in her windows but foliage plants flourished. "I'm glad I've got you guys," she said as she removed a couple of dead leaves.

Opposite the window wall was a closet wall. A third wall had been fitted with standards. Meg had bought brackets and white shelves to hold almost everything she owned. Opposite the shelves was a single bed which she fancied looked like a couch and a small glass coffee table on a colorful rug.

She liked this room, the most cheerful room she'd ever called home.

She lifted a carved wooden walrus with a body as smooth as velvet and rubbed it against her cheek. *What's wrong with this apartment? If we look seriously, Rick and I can find a rental like it. Surely Rick knows that we should rent, not buy. Besides, I won't have money for a down payment until my school debts are paid. I've told Rick that.*

When she had eaten her dinner, she worked conscientiously until eleven o'clock when she watched the news before she slept. Rick did not phone.

When Rick called Tuesday evening, he did not say where he had gone Monday evening and Meg did not ask. Instead, she asked about the long Fourth of July weekend.

"I have to go to Stonefield again but I assumed you'd have to work on Friday, I plan to be back Saturday so we can have Sunday together."

"But I *don't* have to work Friday the fifth."

"Oh? I had supposed you'd be so busy with your mystery client . . ."

"That's moving pretty slowly right now."

"Something going wrong?"

"No. It takes time."

"I could ask what takes time, but—"

"Don't ask, Rick."

"Well, then. Do you want to go to Stonefield? Aunt Hat was in a dither when I told her you wouldn't be able to make it. She said you'd written a lovely note. She says you're a well-bred young lady. That is Aunt Hat's highest accolade."

"Of course I want to go to Stonefield." Meg was puzzled. "Is there some reason you'd rather I stayed in this steaming city, Rick?"

"Oh no, dear. It's just that I'll probably be playing golf with Ran. Maybe having dinner with him . . . The Webster account is hanging."

"I'd better not play golf then—you're both out of my league—but I could try to charm him off the fairway . . ."

"That won't be necessary."

"Then I'll dig in the dirt, which is what I'd rather do anyway. Oh Rick, I do so want to get away from the city for a few days. Are you sure Miss Pearce won't mind? I could stay at the bed-and-breakfast opposite the beaver pond."

"That you cannot do. Aunt Hat would be insulted. Okay, love, I'll call her and tell her we'll be up late tomorrow night. I'll pick you up in front of your building at six-thirty. We'll have dinner on the way up."

"Aunt Hat goes to bed with the birds," Rick said as he turned off the bumpy road into a lane leading to the A-frame. "We'll stop at Piet's to pick up a key for you. Want to come in? He doesn't know one wine from another but he might have some fairly decent beer."

Meg stood in Piet's lane, threw back her head and breathed deeply while the brothers greeted one another. The night was enchanted, warm with fresh pine- and rose-scented breezes. The sky was dotted with stars. Baroque music wafted through the screen door.

"Hi, Meg." Piet spoke slowly and softly. "When I

heard you were coming, I ordered this night just for you. You like it?"

"Oh, I do indeed. It's perfect," she whispered as she stepped to the door and kissed Rick's brother on the cheek.

"Thank you," he said and then led her into the lofty room to their left. He offered them neither wine nor beer, but iced herbal tea and oatmeal cookies, which were laid out on the coffee table, a highly polished cross section of an enormous tree trunk.

While Meg sipped her tea, she looked around her and smiled broadly. "I like your home, Piet." The triangular end wall was made entirely of large panes of glass, some of which were open. Bookcases were built into the sloping side walls. The floors were polished wood except for an area of slate around the freestanding stove. "This is where you were raised, Rick?"

He nodded and pointed to the loft over the kitchen, bathroom, and bedroom. "Piet and I slept up there. Hot in the summer and cold in the winter. Piet's made some improvements since I sold him my half-interest in the house." He pointed to the ceiling fan as one of the improvements.

"While we're on the subject of real estate, Fred, I want you to look over the property you say you want to sell me." Piet spoke firmly.

"You didn't get the paperwork done?" Rick's blue eyes flashed with anger. "You don't have the check?"

"I have both but I don't want to sign either until you have looked at the land. If you want to sell your birthright, I'm prepared to buy it—for considerably more than a bowl of porridge. But you've got to know what you are doing before you do it."

"Are you selling land, Rick? Why?" Meg was bewildered.

"You didn't tell her?" Piet shook his head slowly from side to side.

"Meg's not interested in two acres of land up here."

"Nevertheless, I will not sell it until you look at it, both of you. Tomorrow morning?"

The brothers faced one another, neither of them moving a muscle. Meg studied the two of them. Rick looked small, almost delicate, beside Piet, whose striped polo shirt did nothing to hide his broad chest and shoulders. Dreamboat, his classmates had called him. Rick was Heartthrob. *Unoriginal, but appropriate.*

Rick broke the silence. "I'm tired and so is Meg, so if you'll just hand over the key, I'll take her to Aunt Hat's."

Piet took a key from his pocket and gave it to Rick. Then he turned to Meg. "You will be here tomorrow morning to look at the land, won't you, Meg?" She nodded. "Miss Pearce sleeps downstairs in what used to be the formal parlor. Please turn off the light before you go upstairs. If she wakens and sees the light out, she'll know you've arrived." He turned to Rick. "I'll leave the door open for you but I'll probably be in bed. I'll see you in the morning."

"I have a date to play golf at eleven." Rick sounded petulant.

"Can you be here by nine?" Piet asked Meg.

Rick said nothing as they walked to the car. Nor

did he speak while driving the hundred yards or so to Miss Pearce's lane. When he had stopped the car, he did not turn off the motor but started to open the door.

"Just a minute, Rick. Tell me why you are selling land that seems to me yours. Shouldn't we discuss it?"

"I don't need two measly acres up here on the edge of nowhere."

"How do you happen to own the land?"

"Aunt Hat's father gave my father five acres as a wedding present. Dad built the A-frame on it. When he died, the property passed to Piet and me jointly. A couple of years ago Piet decided that he wanted to be the sole owner of the house. I would have been willing to sell out my entire interest at the time but no, Piet insisted that I keep two acres. Piet's big on telling me what I should do and how I should think . . . When I called him a couple of days ago, I told him that if he wouldn't buy my two acres I'd sell to someone else." Rick laughed. "Poor old Piet. I wonder if he remembered that they have five-acre zoning here now. Only someone who owned land adjacent to my two acres would be interested in them."

"Oh Rick, you wouldn't overcharge him for the land?"

He kissed her nose. "No, my dear, I would not cheat my brother or anyone else. You must know that."

Meg's apprehension melted as fast as it had gathered. "Of course I know that, Rick." She rubbed her cheek against his and they kissed—once. "The five acres should be kept together. It was generous of you to sell your birthright to him." She raised her lips again but he had turned away and was stepping out of the car.

Before she turned off the light, Meg took a peek into the garden room. It was even lovelier than she had remembered, with moonlight spreading a silver sheen on the plants in the windows. Upstairs she was welcomed by a bouquet of miniature roses that had been arranged in a teacup and placed on the washstand that served as a night table. She stood at the window for a long time listening to the night noises and looking out over the dim outlines of the gardens. She forced herself not to think of the sounds of the city and the "view" of a brick wall from the Fifth Avenue apartment windows.

When, at last, she climbed into bed, she tried to think of Rick, not the land he was planning to sell. Of course it was silly for a young man in the city to hang on to land in the country, especially when his own brother wanted to buy it. Selling the land was sensible—and generous.

Chapter Five

MEG opened her eyes, checked the clock, and jumped out of bed. Ten minutes later she was downstairs searching for Miss Pearce. She found her sitting on her golf cart while she cut the dead blooms from the peonies.

"Good morning, Miss Pearce," Meg called. "Thank you for the invitation. I hope I didn't disturb you last—"

"Piet said you and Frederick were going to look over the two acres before his golf game this morning, so you'd better be on your way. Will you be playing golf, too?"

"Not I. I'm hoping you'll have a job for me when I get back."

"Glad you're here, girl. Now hurry."

As she approached the A-frame, Piet stepped out of the door with two mugs of steaming coffee. He handed one of them to her.

Rick, his hair disheveled and his eyes still heavy with sleep, came out and gave her a quick hug. "Hi, pretty lady. I want to apologize for my brother, the slave driver." He grinned at his brother. Last night's tension was gone.

The three of them strolled along the gravel lane to the back of the A-frame. Piet pointed to the features that marked the boundaries of Rick's land—the road at the front and the drive on one side.

"As you can see, I've been using Fred's land," Piet said to Meg, pointing to beds of small plants set out in straight rows. "With his permission. Our dad laid out the beds; I keep them full of nursery stock."

"Look at that!" Rick exclaimed, walking ahead of them to the middle vehicle in an open shed. "What do you call it?"

"I call it my Do-aller." Piet chuckled. "I dig holes with the backhoe—and move trees and rocks. The front loader on the other end is for moving soil or peat moss or whatever from where it is to where I need it. In the winter I convert my Do-aller to a snow blower. It is one terrific piece of machinery."

"And it must have cost you a junior fortune." Rick's brow was furrowed as he peered at his brother.

Piet shrugged. "It's paying for itself." He patted his Do-aller and led them up a steep path to a huge oak. "This marks the end of your property, Rick. But step over here. Wouldn't this be a great place to build a house? You can see into New York State from up here."

The view was spectacular. In the foreground were Piet's planting beds and then his house and Miss Pearce's gardens and house. Across the road, the land fell away sharply into a deep valley with lush green fields and a few white houses and red barns. Beyond the valley, hills rose like waves, ranging in color from dark green to pale violet.

"Oh, Rick." Meg sighed. "It's breathtaking."

"You'd have to acquire more land—another three acres—if you were to build here, but I've spoken to Miss Pearce and she says that if you want to—"

"I don't want to." Rick interrupted his brother. "The land means something to you, Piet, but it means nothing to me. I think of it in terms of all the weeds I had to hoe as a boy."

"I think of it in terms of the trees I planted."

"So let's sign the papers."

"We have to have two witnesses. We'll take them to Laura and Jerry tomorrow morning."

"Fine. I've got to get to the club." He paused in front of Meg and scratched his head. "I . . . ah . . . don't know . . . I'm afraid I'll be gone all day, perhaps late into the night. Ran has invited me back to the cottage, as he calls it. Tennis. Can't afford to—"

"Forget it, Rick." Meg laughed at Rick's discomfort. "I'm going to have a happy day helping Miss Pearce and then I'm going to read. A children's book, I hope. Do you know how long it has been since I read anything I didn't have to read?" She brushed her lips across his. "Have a good time, and don't worry about me. Remember, you didn't ask me to come; I asked myself." She turned to Piet. "Do you have time to tell me about the plants in the beds? What are they? What are you going to do with them? How long have they been growing?" She walked off with Piet.

"Good-bye, Meg," Rick called.

She waved to him while she spoke to Piet. "Poor Rick can't even take a vacation on the Fourth of July. He works so hard."

"I know. He always has."

"So do I. We're wonderfully well suited. But this weekend I am not going to do one thing I don't want to do. I didn't even bring my legal folders with me. So what are these tiny little sprigs that look like pine trees?"

"Pine trees. Dwarfs. Grown-up, they'll be much fuller but only about this high." He pointed to his knee and went on to show her other dwarf conifers with names like 'Gentsch White', and 'Howells Dwarf Tiger Tail'. "This one is a dwarf Douglas fir called *Pseudotsuga menziesii*, 'Graceful Grace'."

"That's a very long name for such a little plant." Meg laughed. "Learning the names of your plants is like learning a foreign language, isn't it?"

He shook his head. "More like learning the names of your friends. This little guy is called 'Coles Prostrate'. I inherited him from my father. I could have sold him I don't know how many times, but he's my buddy. He's given me pieces of himself to root. I buy most of my young plants but I start a few extra special ones myself."

He led her on to show her his rhododendrons and azaleas and dozens of young crab apple trees. He told her that he had beds of young yews and junipers on the other side of Miss Pearce's house. "The plants here, close to my house, are my pets."

They stood in silence while Meg looked at the horticultural wonders all around her. At last she sighed. "I told Miss Pearce I wanted to help her in the garden. She must be suspecting my sincerity."

"I doubt it. Just don't stay out in the sun too long. It's going to be a scorcher today. A perfect day to lie in the hammock with your book."

"Is there a hammock? A real hammock?"

"It's on the wall to your right as you enter the garage. You'll find hooks on a pair of maples about fifty feet from the house. It will be shady there all afternoon. Enjoy." Piet led her to an opening between two hemlock trees and to a path that would take her past the secret garden to the house.

Meg dead-headed the peonies that Miss Pearce could not reach from her cart and then the lilacs. She weeded a bed of mostly daylilies. She had thought that all daylilies were orange like the ones that grow beside country roads. She was wrong. Miss Pearce's daylilies were just beginning to bloom. One tall plant had eight-inch flowers, pale yellow with green throats. A short plant had purple flowers so dark they were almost black.

While they were eating their late lunch, Meg asked Miss Pearce about *The Secret Garden.* "I never read it. If your copy is close at hand, I'd like to read it this afternoon, if I may."

"It's always close at hand." Miss Pearce directed her to a shelf in the garden room.

Meg hung the hammock, climbed into it with the book and fell asleep almost instantly. Hours later when she rolled out of the hammock, Miss Pearce was back in her golf cart taking another tour of her gardens. As they headed toward the house, Meg apologized for sleeping away the afternoon.

"You must have needed the sleep. I suspect you work too hard. Do you?"

"Not physically. I sit at a desk most of the day reading and writing boring documents. That's what lawyering is all about, at least at my level in a big corporate firm."

"Really? Perry Mason has such an exciting life." Miss Pearce laughed. "Mysteries are one of my favorite diversions. But let's go in and have a drink. I never drink alone so it's a double treat to have you here, Meg. I've put on a brand-new outfit for this occasion. You may notice that it's just like all my others." She parked the cart under a low roof near the door to the garden room and stepped to the ground with difficulty, leaning heavily on her cane and Meg's arm.

"It's a lovely shade of rose," Meg said, realizing that except for the dress Miss Pearce had worn to the wedding, she had always appeared in outfits of the same style, loose shirts with large patch pockets over baggy pants. Sneakers on her feet. The new outfit was made of a heavy crinkly cotton. The one she had worn earlier in the day had been light blue seersucker.

"The dress I wore to the wedding is the only dress I own. Woman in town made my first coolie suit some thirty years ago. Her niece makes them for me now, two new ones every year. They're comfortable and they simplify my life."

Meg ran upstairs to wash and change her polo shirt. She entered the garden room with Miss Pearce, who was pushing a tea cart in front of her and leaning on it as if it were a walker. When they had tapped their glasses and Meg had proposed a toast to "growing things," the old lady returned to the subject of lawyering.

"You don't like your work?"

"Of course I do," she responded quickly and then she hesitated. "I hope I do. I don't know." Meg sat rigid for a moment as her words seemed to reverberate through the beautiful room. "I've never said that before. I have worked very hard for many years—and accumulated enormous debts—to become an associate in a top law firm. Maybe it's just that the summer has been so hot and the city is so steamy and the case I am involved with now doesn't interest me much. Life will improve in the fall. Now tell me about you and your garden. I hadn't realized how I miss growing things. I have a window full of houseplants but they are a poor substitute for masses of plants in the ground."

"I'll tell you about me and my garden later. Right now I want to hear about you. Before Harvard Law and Smith. Where were you raised?"

"Vermont. Village called Brinton, near Brattleboro."

"By whom?"

Meg rose to stand in a window at the end of the room. "In the beginning, by my mother and father and then by my father. I've been raising myself since the age of seventeen when I entered Smith."

"You seem to have done a good job, Meg."

"Thank you, Miss Pearce. The cleverest thing I ever did was to be in the right place at the right time to meet Rick." She laughed.

"Where was that?"

"In front of the frozen-food case in a grocery store. I let myself be picked up. First and last time."

"I hope you'll always be as happy with him as

you are now, Meg. Come sit down and have another glass of wine and I'll tell you my secrets."

"You don't have to tell me anything that—" Meg patted the woman's shoulder.

"I know. Sometimes I like to think about my youth. I told you that my mother died when I was eight and that Papa and I came here to live." She talked at some length about a childhood that was supremely happy even though she was the recipient of a great deal of pity. "Every time someone would say, 'Oh that poor little motherless child,' I'd be tempted to laugh. The strange thing is that I loved my mother very much." Miss Pearce said that she had gone away to boarding school. She had hated it so much that, at the end of the first term, her father had let her transfer to the local high school.

She went away again to attend Mount Holyoke. During her freshman year she had met an Amherst senior. "My father forbade me to marry him, saying that he was stupid, lazy, and a gold digger. So I married him, and guess what? He was stupid, lazy, and a gold digger." She chuckled as she moved place settings and a platter of cold boneless chicken breasts and snow peas and a bowl of fruit salad from the tea cart to a small table.

While they ate, she told Meg that she and her husband had lived with his grandmother in Boston. "The old lady thought he should look for work. That irritated him. Then she refused to die and leave her money to him, which made him furious. I went to Boston University and he gambled. When he stole the tuition money my father sent to me, I left him. Eventually, when I had earned my degree,

I swallowed my pride and came home. I was welcomed like a prodigal. Never once did my father remind me that he had warned me. That first summer after my return I built the raised herb garden that surrounds the chimneys. I even laid the bricks," she said proudly.

Miss Pearce had worked for General Electric in Pittsfield during the war. After the war, she and her father had traveled through Europe, mostly looking at gardens. In Holland they had hired Hans Graaf. "The three of us built the gardens and the arboretum."

"You have an arboretum? I loved the Smith College arboretum. Where's yours? What's in it?"

Miss Pearce said that she and her father had tried to collect at least one of every tree that would grow on their hillside. Then they added hybrids. "Now Piet and I are collecting some fascinating Japanese maples. An arboretum interests you, Meg?"

She thought a moment. "Yes. When you told me you had an arboretum, I felt like hugging myself. Silly, isn't it?"

"No. And Piet told me a story that made me wish I had gone to the wedding reception." Meg couldn't imagine what the old lady was talking about. "Piet says that you squatted down and pulled grass out of one of his plantings, completely oblivious to that slip of green silk you were wearing. Fred—Rick, whatever he calls himself these days—sees you as a hotshot lawyer. Piet and I see you as a grubby gardener." She laughed heartily and served them each a wedge of cherry pie.

When Meg returned from the kitchen, where she

had put the food in the refrigerator and loaded the dishes into the dishwasher, Miss Pearce announced that she and Piet were going to replace the old markers on all the trees in the arboretum. "It's a big job and we need all the help we can get. If you have a vacation . . ."

"First two weeks of August."

"And if you'd like to help us?"

"Oh, I would! Rick can't take a vacation until fall and I've made no plans for mine." She paused and looked into the old lady's face. "Do you really want me to spend two weeks here, Miss Pearce? I'm a stranger."

"You are not a stranger to me. You are a gardener. I like you, Meg." She rose stiffly to her feet. "This hasn't been much of a Fourth of July for you. No picnic. No fireworks. I go to bed early, and read. You may watch television if you like. Turn off the lights when you go up."

Meg rose and kissed the wrinkled cheek. "Thank you, Miss Pearce. I've enjoyed this Fourth of July and I'm going to bed early too, to read *The Secret Garden*. You didn't keep your husband's name. What became of him?"

"I don't know. He joined the Navy during World War II, but we were divorced by then. I've never heard from or about him, which is just as well. Did I mention that he was very handsome?"

As the old lady talked about her early love, Meg caught a glimpse of the Harriet Pearce of sixty years ago.

The Secret Garden was not what Meg expected. It began in India where a little girl named Mary

Lenox lived with her busy English father and her mother who "cared only to go to parties and amuse herself with gay people. She had not wanted a little girl at all."

Meg read those two sentences from page 1 twice and then she closed the book decisively. If it had been her book, she would have thrown it across the room or out of the window. She had no intention of reading about a child with a negligent mother. Ever. She glared at the foot of the bed and crashed her fist onto the mattress and then she laughed, albeit weakly, and opened the book again.

Skimming quickly through Chapter 1, she came upon the deaths of both of Mary's parents. In Chapter 2, the orphaned Mary returned to England. Meg read straight through to the end.

Chapter Six

FRIDAY was another delicious day. Meg and Miss Pearce were out in the garden early, drinking coffee and eating muffins, and discussing the bratty little orphan Mary Lenox and the hysterical invalid Colin.

"Dickon, the nature boy who talks to animals, is just too good to be true," Meg said critically.

"Right. The book is overly sentimental."

"And I loved it, Miss Pearce. I read parts of it twice before I fell asleep."

"I love it, too. I read it once every year, usually on Christmas Eve. Gardens are healing, you know. This garden healed my father—and me."

Their discussion was interrupted by the arrival of two cars. Miss Pearce's housekeeper and her son, a teenager who mowed the lawns, were in the first car. Piet and Rick were in the second.

"This day is yours," Rick announced to Meg. "Piet and I have to take care of our business and then I'll be back to whisk you off to Williamstown. You'll love the Clark Museum. We'll be eating out," he said to Miss Pearce. "I expect to keep her all to myself until very late." His eyes twinkled suggestively.

Early in the afternoon, Meg and Rick were driving past the Stonefield church. Tour buses clogged the main street. Trucks and vans were parked in an open area at the ends of several of the side streets. Hoards of people spilled out into the road. "What is going on?" Meg asked. "Last time I was here this was a sleepy little town."

"It was always a sleepy town when I was a boy. We used to play in that field behind the town. Now it's an open-air market—produce and crafts. Piet says that tourists flock to town on weekends during the Tanglewood season."

"Tanglewood? How far is it from here? Could we go, Rick?"

He frowned and shook his head and then grinned. "How about the rehearsal tomorrow morning?"

The drive to Williamstown was through rolling hills. They strolled through the Clark Museum and then the streets of the town. Rick showed her where he had lived when he was at Williams College and where he had taken some of his favorite courses. They ate at an acceptable restaurant, drove home slowly, and parked in front of the garage. Rick took her into his arms and kissed her gently . . .

I am a very fortunate woman, Meg said to herself when she finally went into the house.

She woke to hear Miss Pearce calling from the foot of the stairs. She squinted at the clock—it was eight-thirty—and ran down to the old lady, apologizing for sleeping so late.

"Expect you were late getting in. Piet just called to say that if you're going to the rehearsal at Tanglewood this morning, you'd best leave by nine."

"Rick said it doesn't start until ten-thirty."

"Right, but Piet says you have to get there early if you want good seats. He's getting Fred on his feet. Help yourself to breakfast." She turned and limped toward the door, then turned back. "Did you have a good time yesterday, Meg?"

"Oh yes." Meg hugged herself.

"Frederick has always been good company. When he was a little boy, he used to come to the house to chat with my father. Papa loved him so. He said once that he'd never missed having a son until he met Frederick."

"And Piet?" Meg asked.

"Papa undervalued Piet. He isn't as good a talker as his brother but he wears well. Piet enriches my life."

Rick enriches my life, Meg said to herself as she went on to the kitchen to pour herself a mug of coffee.

"You were right, old man," Rick said to Piet as they searched the front rows of the shed at Tanglewood for three empty seats. They'd had to park a distance from the gate and then wait in line for tickets. It was almost ten o'clock and the best seats had been taken. "Thanks for pulling me out of bed when you did. Sorry I wasn't more gracious about it. As you know, this lovely lady kept me up beyond my bedtime." He hugged Meg to him.

When they were settled in the best seats they could find, Meg looked around her. What was called a shed was really a metal roof supported by a maze of steel girders. It protected plain wooden seats on a slanted dirt floor. Beyond the shed were green lawns dotted with blankets, coolers, and people, mostly young. A famous cellist and an even more famous guest conductor would be rehearsing the program for Sunday afternoon.

"When do they practice the program for tonight?" she asked Piet.

"I don't know. They don't invite the public."

"Do you come to Tanglewood often?"

"The Friday evening concert or the rehearsal. One or the other. The other weekend performances are too crowded."

Members of the orchestra, dressed in jeans and polo shirts, straggled onto the stage and tuned their instruments. And then the conductor scurried to the podium. They played straight through the first piece. When the cellist joined them for the next number it was stop and go all the way. Finally they reached the end and stopped for intermission.

Piet pulled a rope out of his pocket and tied it across the three seats they had occupied. Out on the lawn, he pointed to a red house in the distance, the house where Nathaniel Hawthorne had written his *Tanglewood Tales*.

A female voice called Rick's name and they all three turned toward a young woman who placed a tiny hand on Rick's arm. She was not fat but she gave the impression of roundness. She had a round face with a sprinkling of freckles across a nub of a nose, blond hair in shoulder-length ringlets, round breasts above a tiny waist. She looked uncertainly from Meg to Piet.

"Hi, Jocelyn," Rick said easily. "Meet my brother, Piet, and Meg Bower. This is Jocelyn Montgomery." While they were acknowledging the introduction, Rick stepped back. "We're on our way for coffee," he said and then muttered something Meg could not hear.

"See you this afternoon," Jocelyn called as she turned and ran off in the opposite direction.

"I guess I didn't tell you, Meg," Rick said. "Another command performance at Chez Montgomery. Anything to keep the potential client happy." He laughed. "Meg understands these things, Piet."

Piet scowled.

Meg smiled brightly. Of course Rick had to court a potential client. She had no objection to that. She just wished that the client's daughter, if he had to have one, were homely—or much younger or much older.

When the rehearsal ended, they drove back to Stonefield and ate lunch at the open-air restaurant. Rick chatted amusingly. Piet said almost nothing. As they were leaving, Meg announced that she would like to explore Stonefield.

"I'm sorry, darling," Rick said, nuzzling her cheek. "Duty calls. I just have time to shower and change."

"Tell you what." Piet paused. "I'll drive home with you, Rick, and get my truck. I have an appointment to look at an apple orchard this afternoon. Suppose you wander around town, Meg. I'll join you in about half an hour. When you're through in town, I'll drive you to Miss Pearce's or we'll go together to look at the orchard. I think you'll like it, and the people who own it." He hesitated, frowning. "But maybe you'd rather not ride in my rusty old truck . . ."

"Rust matches my hair." She smiled. "And I'd love to see the orchard."

Farmers were selling strawberries and lettuce and peas from the back of trucks. Others were selling flowers and plants. Crafts people had set up tables to display their wares. Meg was selecting a pair of enamel earrings for herself when Piet returned. "Which do you like best?" she asked, holding up two pairs.

He studied them thoughtfully and then the others on display. At last he picked up a pair. "What about these?" he asked.

"You don't think they're too gaudy?"

"Not on you."

"You think I'm gaudy?" She laughed.

He bit his lip and shook his head. "Not gaudy. Vivid. *You* are vivid." He might have added "unlike pale Jocelyn," which is what they were both thinking. "I'd like to buy them for you."

"No. Rick wouldn't . . ."

"Of course." He waited while she paid for her purchase and then walked with her from one display to the next.

"What could I buy Miss Pearce?" she asked.

"Strawberries," he said without hesitation. "She can't get enough during the season. Believe me, she loves strawberries. And so do I. She's invited me to dinner tonight."

Meg bought two quarts of big, luscious-looking berries and a plain cake from a baked-goods table. Piet said they'd buy ice cream on the way home.

Piet's pickup was rusty and the upholstery had been mended with plastic tape, but it seemed to run smoothly. Several miles outside of town he slowed the truck to crawl along the shoulder of the road past rows of ancient apple trees. He turned into a lane that led to a small red house.

A little girl, who had been playing in a sandbox beside the house, jumped up and ran to the lane and carefully positioned both of her feet so that her toes just touched the gravel. "Hi, Mr. Giraffe," she called as the truck pulled to a stop.

"She's forbidden to step into the lane," Piet whispered to Meg as he held the truck door for her. "Alice Berkhardt, meet Miss Bower," he said as they approached the child, who shook hands with both of them.

"Mr. Giraffe is here," the child called to a dark-haired man with black-rimmed glasses who was walking toward them from the house.

"His name is Mr. Graaf, Alice. Mr. Graaf." He smoothed her shiny dark hair.

"Mr. Giraffe." Alice giggled defiantly.

"I like it when Alice calls me Mr. Giraffe. Makes me wish I had a long neck and spots." Piet laughed and then introduced Meg to Dr. Berkhardt, who asked to be called Jack, and then to his wife, Natalie, and a sturdy toddler named Andy.

"I'm afraid the orchard is even sicker than when you saw it last fall," Natalie said mournfully. "You know that we want to save the trees, all of them, if that is possible. Some of them bloomed just as extravagantly as ever this spring."

"I know. I drove past several times during the blooming season. We'll consider them individually."

" 'There is so much individuality of character among apple-trees, that it gives them an additional claim to be the objects of human interest.' " Jack seemed to be quoting.

" 'The variety of grotesque shapes into which apple-trees contort themselves, has its effect on those who get acquainted with them,' " Natalie Berkhardt added. " 'They stretch out their crooked branches, and take such hold of the imagination—' "

" '—that we remember them as humorists and odd fellows,' " Piet concluded with a laugh and then turned to a bewildered Meg. "Nathaniel Hawthorne on the subject of apple trees," he explained.

They set off to walk among the trees. "These two old soldiers have definitely faded away," Jack said.

Piet broke off a slim branch and looked at it. "No sign of life." He took orange plastic ribbon from his pocket and tied a piece on each tree before he hurried on to the next tree to announce that all it needed was a little pruning.

While they walked among the trees, considering each one, Jack swung the toddler onto his shoulders and Alice put her hand in Meg's. "Mommy painted the trees," she said.

Meg had a vision of compact Natalie standing on a ladder to brush colors on each tree. Then she remembered a conversation she had heard at the wedding reception about Natalie, who was going to illustrate the book about the beavers.

"She painted me in one of the pictures, when I was just a little girl. She didn't paint Andy because we didn't have Andy then. Andy's new. The picture's in our winter house. This is our summer house and our Christmas house. I make pictures, too. Do you?"

"No, Alice. I sit in a stuffy office and read boring law books."

When they had completed the tour of the trees, Jack led them to lawn chairs near the house to discuss treatment for the trees that were ill and replacements for those that had died.

"Want to see my river?" Alice asked Meg.

Meg nodded and Alice led her around the house to a path through a strip of woods to a stream.

" 'Dark brown in the river,' " Alice quoted. "My river isn't brown, is it?"

Meg looked at the child, entranced. " 'Golden is the sand,' " Meg whispered. "I loved that poem when I was a child. My father read it to me. 'It goes along forever, with trees on either hand.' "

Alice dropped a stick into the water and they watched it until it disappeared behind a rock.

" 'How would you like to go up in a swing, up in the air so blue?' " Meg said slowly, remembering.

" 'Oh, I do think it's the. . . .' I forget."

" 'Oh, I do think it the pleasantest thing . . .' " Meg prompted.

" 'Ever a child can do!' " Alice shouted triumphantly.

She took Meg's hand and led her back toward the house to a tire swing hung in a huge maple tree. When Meg was seated in the tire, Alice climbed onto her lap and they swung gently to and fro. Meg rested her head on the child's head and held her snug in her arms.

Meg's elder niece and her nephew, both towheads, had been just as dear at this age, loved and loving. She wondered if they were still so blond. Her younger niece was a redhead. She hadn't seen her since she was a toddler. Holding Alice in her arms, she felt a renewed longing to see her brother and his children. If only Brinton were not haunted by the ghost of another little girl, Meg herself.

She shook the ghost from her brain and shoved her heel against the ground to move the clumsy swing. Alice wrapped her arms around Meg's neck and laughed joyfully.

"So, Miss Alice," Meg said, "tell me about your life. You draw and you listen to stories and poems. What else do you do? Do you take care of a doll?"

Alice nodded. "Her name is Tooley. And I build with blocks and when we go back to our winter house I am going to go to school, not every day but some days. Andy can't go to school because he's too little."

"He'll miss you while you're gone," Meg said. "Poor Andy."

"Poor Andy," Alice repeated, leaning back to grin up at Meg. Alice was obviously not wasting her sympathy on her little brother.

They were still sitting in the swing, chatting like old friends, when Piet came to find them. Alice followed them to the edge of the lane and stood waving until they turned onto the main road.

"Thank you, Piet." Meg sighed. "I don't see little

children very often but Alice is my idea of a ten among kids. She's so bright. She was quoting from *A Child's Garden of Verses* and she's only three years old."

"She's something, isn't she?" He turned to grin at Meg. "So are the other members of her family. Jack's a professor at MIT."

Back at Miss Pearce's, Meg changed into her work clothes and weeded a perennial garden, delighting in the fragrance of new-mown grass.

When Piet arrived for dinner, he brought a copy of *A Child's Garden of Verses,* illustrated by Natalie. He opened it to show Meg the page opposite the title page, which had been filled with a penned picture of a kindly giraffe and these words: "To our dear friend, Piet Graaf, who loves all growing things, with affection from Natalie."

"You must treasure this," Meg said. "I'll be careful with it and return it tomorrow."

When they had stuffed themselves with cold beef, salad, and strawberry shortcake, Meg and Piet went to the kitchen to load the dishwasher.

"I've enjoyed this day, Piet, the concert and Alice and the apple trees. Thank you." She put her hand on his arm.

He looked down at her hand for just a moment before he pulled his arm away from her and hurled a sponge into the sink. He mumbled good-bye to her, shouted to Miss Pearce to let her know he was going, and strode to the door and out of the house.

Meg stood in the middle of the kitchen, shaking her head, bewildered. What had she said to offend Piet?

Chapter Seven

It was raining so hard on Sunday morning that Rick called from Piet's to suggest that they head back to the city as soon as they finished breakfast. It was still pouring when they turned onto the southbound highway.

"Piet sounded mighty enthusiastic about his afternoon and evening with you yesterday. And you? Did you have a good time too, Meg?" Rick's tone was testy.

Meg's shoulders stiffened as she turned to stare at Rick's profile. Did he mistrust her with his brother? Absurd. She took a deep breath. "We had a very pleasant afternoon. We walked around the farmers' market and then we went to see what could be done about an ancient apple orchard. The owners obviously respect Piet. He's a professor at MIT."

"My, my, but the old town *is* getting classy," Rick inserted.

"His wife is a children's book illustrator."

He shrugged as if to say, "So what?"

"Their elder child is a darling. Her name is Alice. She calls Piet Mr. Giraffe. She quotes poetry and she's only three. They have a little boy, too. And a red house and—"

"Then what did you do?"

"I weeded for a little while and we had a late dinner. Piet came for dinner. Beef. I bought strawberries and a cake and ice cream for dessert."

"Good move. Aunt Hat likes strawberries. Then you and Piet . . . ?"

"Piet went home right after dinner. He loaned me a copy of *A Child's Garden of Verses*. I had a copy of it when I was a child but Piet's is a new edition, illustrated by Natalie. I read it, with great pleasure. And then I started a novel I'd brought with me. It put me to sleep." She bit her tongue for a moment and then spoke through clenched teeth. "Is that report sufficiently detailed?"

He shrugged but said nothing.

Meg sat rigidly while the swish-swish of the windshield wipers punctuated the silence. Finally, she voiced the question that she could not silence. "Why don't you tell me what *you* did Thursday morning, afternoon, and evening? Yesterday afternoon and evening."

"Hell, Meg. You know that I'm courting Montgomery. It's business. Strictly business."

"Does Miss Montgomery know that? Does she know you are engaged? At Tanglewood yesterday, I wondered if you might not be passing me off as your brother's girl."

Rick was silent a moment and then he laughed and tickled her under the chin. "A few minutes ago the green-eyed monster bit me. And now he's biting you. That will never do, will it, darling?"

She tried to laugh with him but her shoulders still felt stiff. "No, Rick, it will never do." She paused a minute. "Were you really jealous of your brother?"

"Were you really jealous of Jocelyn Montgomery?"

"I guess I was, a little. Incidentally—or not so incidentally—you're going to have to trust me with your brother. I'll be spending my vacation with Miss Pearce and Piet. We're going to work in the arboretum."

"You're going to what? Hike around in those gloomy woods for days on end? I did that one summer when I was in high school. Let me tell you it is boring, boring, boring. You'll hate it. Why didn't you put her off until you'd had a chance to talk to me about it? Oh Meg, I asked you to try to endear yourself to Aunt Hat, but not at the expense of your vacation. You can drop her a note or phone. Tell her your vacation's been changed to the winter months or that you've just been invited to a castle in Spain. She won't like it but she won't hold a grudge. She never does."

"I want to spend my vacation that way, Rick. I like Miss Pearce and her home and her gardens."

"And Piet?"

"And Piet."

They rode on in silence until suddenly Rick threw back his head. "Thank the Lord," he shouted. "We are entering the Bronx and soon we'll be back in good old Manhattan, the home of the doers and shakers of the world. Let's pick up the *Times* and study the ads and go look at a few apartments. Shall we?"

"It's too late. Any bargain rentals in today's paper are gone by now."

"I was thinking of co-ops, not rentals."

"I don't want to buy an apartment, Rick. Someday I want a house with a garden and room for children."

"Come off it, Meg. You don't want to commute, and I thought we both agreed that we were too busy to be bothered with children."

"You did the agreeing on that, Rick."

"You can't even think about a child until you've got your partnership and that's another four years. In the meantime, we can buy a pleasant one-bedroom apartment convenient to our offices."

"With what?"

"I have some money with my broker and now I have the check from Piet. Minimum down payment. We make enough to support a substantial mortgage."

"I don't. Not until my debts are paid. I don't want to own property in the city, not yet."

"You're being positively obstructionist, Meg. I'll never take you to Stonefield again; not if this is the way it affects you. What *do* you want to do this afternoon?"

She thought and then spoke the truth, knowing that it would irritate him. "I want to go home, do my laundry, clean my room, read the *Times*, and watch a little television. I'll also give myself a much-needed manicure." She put her hand on the steering wheel to show him her grimy broken nails. "Miss Pearce gave me a pair of garden gloves but I took them off and forgot to put them back on."

He took his eyes from the road just long enough to look at her. "I can't believe this," he said, tapping his finger across her nails. "You have beautiful hands, patrician hands. How could you let them look like they belonged on the arms of a peasant?"

"Maybe I am a peasant," she challenged.

"You are a bright, sophisticated lawyer," he said through clenched teeth. "I don't know why you have to be alone to work on your hands but if you don't want me around, I'll stay away. I have a memo to write. I may even write to my mother." He *was* angry. "I thought that loving me you liked to spend time with me."

She said nothing until he pulled into the bus stop in front of her building and then she simply said that she was sorry.

He grinned, semiconvincingly. "Do your own thing, Meg. I'll phone you on Tuesday to test the waters. I hope they'll be considerably warmer than they are now."

"I hope so, too." She took her bag and hurried inside.

For reasons she did not fully understand, Meg felt like an overstretched rubber band, ready to snap. When she'd returned from Stonefield the day after the wedding, she'd felt refreshed, happy, tranquil. Why didn't she feel that way this time? It was a question she preferred not to consider.

She gathered her dirty clothes and loaded them

into two machines in the dreary basement of her building. Waiting for her wash to complete its cycles, she perched on an old kitchen table with her back against gray painted bricks.

If only she had thought to go out for the paper before she started the wash. As it was, she had nothing to do but think. *And heaven knows I don't want to think*, she said to herself. It was a fate she could not avoid. She kneaded her neck and shoulders, hoping to relax them while she tried to review the happy parts of her weekend.

Thursday, the Fourth, had been a delight. While Rick worked, Meg had become better acquainted with Miss Pearce. She was well on the way to loving that brusque old lady. They'd had a wonderful conversation. *Censor.* Some segments of the conversation were better left unexamined.

Rick had spent the day with the Montgomeries. He was courting the father for business purposes. Of course the daughter was present in her father's house. She was tiny and cute—two adjectives that had *never* been applied to Meg—and had put her little hand on Rick's arm. So what?

Meg had enjoyed every moment of her Friday with Rick. She always enjoyed being with Rick. He was so sophisticated and competent. He made her feel special. He was unlike anyone she had ever known and he had chosen her. She was one lucky lady. So why didn't she want to spend this afternoon with him? How could she have chosen her laundry over him?

Saturday, she had met Alice and the apple trees. Was Alice responsible for Meg's discomfort? While she was considering that question, she moved her clothes to the dryer. Alice had been a delight for one hour but surely she was not endearing all of the time. Meg tried to picture her in the throes of a tantrum, kicking her feet and screeching, her face blotchy and tear-streaked. The picture should have disgusted Meg; instead it made her laugh.

She hung the quick-to-dry things on hangers and went on thinking about Alice in particular and children in general. Rick hadn't said they'd never have a child, just that they'd postpone parenthood until she had her partnership. That wasn't unreasonable. Babies were created by two people, both of whom should want them. Did most men want to have children? She'd try to find the answer to that question.

As she folded the rest of her laundry, she reviewed her previous thoughts, congratulating herself on her methodical and practical problem-solving. Rick and she had both been jealous but they both knew that the foundations of their jealousy were nonexistent. So why didn't they kiss and make up? Because they were on a fast-moving highway in a torrential rainstorm. And then Rick had dismissed her suggestion that they consider—just consider—a house with a garden, and a baby. Was that what made her so tense? The fact that he was single-mindedly pursuing his dream of owning an apartment in a "good" neighborhood. Was that all?

It was not, and she knew it was not. She waited until she was upstairs, putting her clean sheets on her bed, before she forced herself to review the conversation she had had with Miss Pearce on July Fourth. Miss Pearce had asked her if she liked her work. Meg tugged at a corner of the bottom sheet until it popped over the corner of the mattress and then she sat down and buried her face in her hands. *Do I like my work? No, I do not.*

Although most young people who didn't like what they were doing could simply change to another field, for Meg the admission was cataclysmic. One summer, at an inn where she was working, Meg had talked at some length with one of the guests, a woman who had studied to be a surgeon only to discover that she hated the detail and pressure of her work and her emotional distance from her patients. She was good, she said, with a "brilliant future," but she left in the middle of her residency to become a country doctor in a little town in Idaho. Meg had been baffled by the woman. Why didn't she know what kind of doctoring she wanted to do before she began her intensive training? Having won a coveted residency at Mass. General, she owed it to her superiors and herself—and certainly to other women—to carry through. Meg had never dreamed that she herself could be in a similar situation.

She wasn't. She'd made a choice; she'd stick with it. She reached for her calculator. Sixty hours a week for 50 weeks is 3,000 hours a year, times 35 years, is over one hundred thousand hours. *Cut the melodrama, Meg. You chose law, freely, with no pressure from anyone.*

She finished making her bed and put her clean clothes away, and thought about her choice. She had entered Smith as an English major with vague plans to teach. During her freshman year she had begun to think about publishing and advertising.

During her junior year, a classmate's brother was hired, straight out of Harvard Law, at a salary that was more than twice what a first-year teacher could make in the most affluent suburb. Meg was impressed by the money but she knew that she could never stand up in court to defend the innocent with emotional speeches and sudden bursts of intuition. She laughed at her vision, which was based solely on television and the movies. Eventually she'd discovered that not all lawyers do trial work. She began to cherish the historical roots of the law, the Magna Carta, the Constitution, the idea of equal justice for all. Many famous men were lawyers, and a few famous women. It was a noble calling and Meg had embraced it enthusiastically.

So what's ailing me now? Her work had begun to seem trivial, unworthy of the long hours. When had she first begun to feel this way? Last year? Was it only mergers and acquisitions that bored her? If so, she could ask for a transfer. With that happy thought, she ran out to buy the *Times* and a deli sandwich for her supper.

She and Blythe bumped umbrellas as they ran into the building from opposite directions. "I want to ask you a personal question," Meg said as they rode up in the elevator. "It's sort of a research project. I'll make us iced tea."

Blythe looked surprised. Although she had been instrumental in changing Meg from drab to chic, the two had never shared confidences. Nevertheless, she nodded her agreement and went to hang her red slicker in the bathroom. She returned wearing a black and white cotton shirt over nothing that Meg could see. Her hair was even blacker than usual. Her chalky white skin was punctuated by heavy black lashes and brows and a vivid red mouth. She reminded Meg of a harlequin.

"Do you like your job?" Meg asked as they settled on the floor, leaning back against the side of her bed. "Do you think most people go to work happily on Monday mornings?"

"I love my job," Blythe said without hesitation. "I wish it paid better, but every morning—well, almost every morning—I get up happy to be going to my office to meet interesting people in dramatic clothes. Tomorrow we're going to be shooting furs for the December issue."

"Furs? In this heat? You want to stand around and watch poor innocent models die of heat stroke?"

"They won't die. As for my friends, many of them are actors or dancers or musicians. If they are working in their fields, they are happy. If not, if they're just working to earn money, they are not happy, but most of them have dreams to sustain them. That's what's so great about New York. The dreams."

Blythe sat silently, obviously thinking of "the dreams," and then she continued. "My father worked on an assembly line, except during layoffs and strikes, all the time we were growing up. I don't suppose he ever really liked his work, but he loved his wife and his kids and he worked to support us. I imagine that he is more typical than the people I know. Do you like your work, Meg?"

"I don't know. That's what I'm trying to find out."

"And that gorgeous man of yours? Does he like his work?"

"Yes, he does, but . . ." Meg did not finish the sentence.

Blythe looked at her closely, drained her glass and went to her own room.

Chapter Eight

MONDAY morning Meg stepped out of her building onto a sidewalk washed clean by the rain. The sky was cloudless. The air was warm and dry. It was the perfect summer day, a day for relaxing and rejoicing. Meg, still tense, could do neither.

She looked into the faces of the strangers coming toward her as she walked to the bus. Were they happy to be going to work? Some were. A very properly dressed middle-aged man strode along swinging his briefcase and whistling. Meg laughed when she recognized the tune: It was the song the dwarfs in *Snow White* sang when they went off to work.

Most people ambled along, as if resigned to their fate, but some seemed utterly miserable. A little boy was being dragged along the sidewalk by his angry mother. The bus driver hated the bus, the passengers, the cars and trucks that crowded the streets—and himself too, probably.

During the long, boring day, Meg phoned a former Smith College roommate and close friend, Amy Atkins, now Grant. At seven o'clock she left the office with a gaily wrapped box holding a fuzzy rabbit so soft and cuddly that Meg would have liked to have kept it herself.

She went down into the steam-bath subway and twenty minutes later was walking out into the open air of Jackson Heights in Queens. Amy lived on a tree-lined street in a small building, one of twelve built around a garden that Meg could just glimpse from the sidewalk. Civilized, she proclaimed to herself, a practical compromise between cement city and grassy suburb. Everything Amy did was practical, sensible.

Amy greeted her warmly. "Come and see him. He is so absolutely the most beautiful . . . But I'm his mother. I shouldn't say that, should I?"

Amy? Cool, practical, sensible Amy, babbling like a press agent on behalf of an infant? Meg couldn't believe the change in her friend as she was led into a nursery where a tiny baby slept with his bottom up in the air.

"He is beautiful," Meg said. "Absolutely beautiful." Before they left the nursery, Meg stepped over to the window to look out into the garden with lawn and ivy growing among mature trees. "It's like having your own backyard, isn't it, Amy?"

"Except that we share it with a hundred other families—which is both good and bad."

Amy's husband was visiting a sick relative, and Amy had prepared salads that they ate in the kitchen. "So what's the problem?" she asked as soon as they had begun to eat.

"Do you like your work, Amy?"

"If you mean mothering, the answer is an emphatic yes. I expect that I will eventually find it a bit isolating, but right now I love it. You just cannot imagine how interesting Brian is. If you mean accounting, the answer is sometimes yes, sometimes no. It's not exactly a thrill a minute but I get satisfaction out of numbers that balance. Right now I like it because I can work here at home while Brian sleeps. Later, when he doesn't sleep so much, I'll hire someone to take him to the park for a few hours a day."

"And your husband? Was he as enthusiastic about having a baby as you are?"

"Heavens no. I think he only agreed to it to please me—and his mother. His mother was dying to be a grandmother. But now? I wish you could see him. He thinks the whole thing was his idea and that Brian is the best-looking, most intelligent child in the world." Amy sobered. "So why are you asking these questions, Meg? Does that handsome Rick say he doesn't want to have children? Just tell him that anyone with his looks owes it to the human race to sire at least a dozen children."

Meg laughed. Amy's argument would appeal to Rick. "It's more than that. It's my job." Meg went on to describe the work she did, the hours she spent reading dull cases and writing duller documents. "I'm going to ask for a transfer to another department, but what if I don't like that, either? That worries me."

"Why don't you wait to worry until you've tried another position?"

"Why don't I? What made you so sensible, Amy?"

She shrugged. "Remember this: you didn't exactly love waiting tables but you did it, for years. You needed the money."

"You're right. I was actually a very good waitress."

"And you earned fantastic tips, as I recall."

Meg leaned back in her chair, relaxed at last, and smiled at her friend. "I miss you, Amy. You make me feel like one of your financial records, balanced. Thank you."

The next day, Tuesday, Meg spoke to Mr. Spencer about transferring to another department. "I'd like to broaden my experience, before I settle into my lifetime area of expertise."

"That's probably a good idea. Would you want to float for a while? It's not generally thought to be the path to a partnership but . . . They need a temporary in trusts. Right away."

"Thank you. I'd like that."

"It'll only be for a couple of weeks. I'll put the word out that you are available to other departments, but I hope you'll be back in our stable very soon. We have high hopes for you, Meg."

When Rick called that evening, Meg reported happily on the change in her career.

"You're leaving mergers and acquisitions? Now? Has something happened to the case you were working on?"

"No. Joel's handling it. He thinks it's fascinating. I'm sorry I was a pain on Sunday, Rick."

Wednesday, Meg was put to work writing a will more complicated than anything she had encountered in law school. The testator had millions of dollars. He also had a mother, three ex-wives, one current wife, nine children, and three stepchildren. The children ranged in age from thirty-seven to four. One son had already gone through more money than any three of the other children combined. The testator wanted to leave a substantial sum to his college. And then there were the grandchildren, the six that had been born and who-knew-how-many yet to be born. Above all, he wanted to be fair, which meant leaving more money to the younger children—who had not yet been educated—than to the older children who had. How much more?

She worked diligently every day and late every night. To her surprise, she was enjoying her work. It had all the drama of a novel. Humor too, unlike the papers they had been filing for Dixon.

She did not see Rick until Saturday evening when they went to South Street Seaport. Not a cross word passed the lips of either of them.

Sunday, when Rick suggested they look at apartments, she reminded him that she did not wish to buy either a co-op or a condo. He readily agreed to look at rentals and they both remained good-humored. "Rather small," Meg said about one that was the size of a broom closet.

"A first-class co-op might be cheaper," Rick said about one that rented for more than the national average income.

They were infinitely polite when they met for dinner during the following week. Saturday Meg had to work so Rick spent the day with friends in the Hamptons. They met late Sunday afternoon for a walk through the park and dinner on the West Side.

Their relationship was just as it had been before the July Fourth weekend, Meg told herself. The only difference was that she was happier with her work. Her life was wonderful. Just wonderful. She loved Rick and he loved her and they were going to have a beautiful life together.

He called her on Monday to tell her to get out her "fancy duds" for a yacht party on Wednesday.

"I thought you had to go to Chicago on Wednesday. Will the green silk do?"

"I'll leave early Thursday morning. The green silk? Maybe you can dress it up. I'll be wearing a dinner jacket."

"Right. I'll wear my diamonds." She hesitated. "Unless you think they might be a bit ostentatious for a boating party. Perhaps the emeralds, or . . . I'll just have to see what's in the vault, dahling."

"Cut the humor, Meg. This is important. The president of the agency has asked me to represent him."

"That's an honor, Rick," she said seriously. "What's the occasion?"

"A benefit for a school on one of the islands in the Caribbean. I can't remember which one."

"A benefit in July? Anyone who reads the *Times* knows that all the beautiful people are in the Hamptons in July. No one would give a benefit now."

"Except Mr. S. J. Solitario, who is the president of Solitario, Inc., a good client of ours. He has a place on the island and is the chief sponsor of a school that was destroyed by fire two weeks ago. So he's bringing his yacht and some local talent to New York and asking his quote friends unquote to rebuild the school. The account exec and his wife and a couple of others from the agency will be there. Our president bought the tickets, but . . . rumor has it that his wife is not an asset businesswise. She spends her summers in some out-of-the-way place in Maine making dulcimers. He's up there now but he called me—or rather his secretary did—this morning."

"The wife of the president of one of the top agencies in New York City makes dulcimers? Maybe he likes dulcimers too, and out-of-the-way places. I'll bet she has a garden. She may even make pickles." Meg laughed. "Do they have children?"

"Six of them. Rumor has it they're all as crazy as their mother. One is spending a year on a sheep farm in Australia. Another is someplace in Africa with some do-good organization."

"And all these crazy kids have the same father and mother who have been married for many years. That's extraordinary these days, isn't it, Rick? I think I'd like the president of your agency—and his wife."

Once again, Blythe came through and loaned Meg a beaded bolero to wear over the green silk. It made Meg feel like a Christmas tree ornament, but Rick loved it.

Meg, who had never been on a yacht before, was wonderstruck. A calypso band played on the top deck. The rum drinks were garnished with fresh fruits. The buffet table was set with exotic foods. The plea for money was understated but effective. Rick presented her to his business associates as if she were a special treat.

Late in the evening, Meg and Rick stood against the railing, isolated from the others, and listened to the waves lapping against the sides of the boat as they gazed at the lighted Manhattan skyline. It was a magical moment, standing there with Rick's arms around her.

She worked Saturday morning and spent the rest of the weekend missing Rick, who was off at his convention in Chicago.

He phoned just as she was leaving for work on Tuesday morning. It was hot in Chicago but he'd hardly left the convention hotel where he was making some good contacts and attending dull meetings. He hadn't had a minute to phone her earlier. "But I'll be home soon. Are you still determined to waste your vacation on Aunt Hat's arboretum?"

"I don't think it will be a waste of time. I'm looking forward to communing with the trees for two weeks. I just wish you were coming, too."

"You know I can't get away. Too many irons in the fire. But come December . . . And I'll drive you to Stonefield Saturday. I've heard about an inn in Connecticut. We'll stop there for lunch."

"I won't see you until Saturday?" Meg cursed the wistful tone in her voice.

"I'm sorry, darling. It's just that I'll have all these reports to write when I get back to the office. That's the great thing about you, Meg, you understand business demands. I have to run . . . a business breakfast. Till Saturday."

Meg replaced the receiver and rubbed the back of her neck. For days she'd been waiting for a call from Rick. After his call, she still felt dissatisfied. It wasn't anything he had said. He didn't care about the arboretum, but that was of no significance. They didn't have to love the same things to love one another. No, it wasn't the arboretum. She couldn't define her uneasy feeling.

Chapter Nine

SATURDAY morning, Rick stowed her bags in the trunk and held the car door for her. Then he kissed her sweetly. He kissed her again before he fastened his seat belt.

He had little to say about his trip to Chicago except that the weather had been hot and muggy. Meg couldn't tell him about the will she had written without giving details that might identify the client. Conversation, mostly about the scenery, was sporadic, so the trip seemed long.

When at last they pulled into a parking lot shaded by huge maples, Meg sprang from the car as soon as it came to a stop. She wished she could walk around outside the white clapboard inn for a few minutes, but Rick was eager to enter. Their table, in front of an open window looking out on flawless lawns and clipped hedges, was set with fresh flowers, pink linen, and stemmed crystal. As soon as they were seated, Rick reached across the table to lift her hand to his lips.

A waiter arrived with a wine cooler and a split of

champagne. "Our finest French," he said, showing the label to Rick. Rick examined it suspiciously and at last nodded. The waiter popped the cork and splashed a little into Rick's chilled glass. Rick sipped it thoughtfully and nodded again. When both glasses had been filled and the waiter had faded away, they lifted their glasses.

"To us and our love," Rick said, looking deep into her eyes.

"To us," she repeated. It was like a scene from a movie. She giggled. "Are we celebrating something?"

He reached into his blazer pocket. Panicked, she felt her blood rushing to her head. Her hand shook as she placed her napkin beside her plate and started to rise. And then she laughed. What he had taken from his pocket was not a ring but a small book. She sighed and sat back in her chair. Her relief was short-lived.

"Pick the day," he said, handing her the date book. "I've thought about us a lot since that dismal Sunday after the Fourth. We've been engaged long enough. It's time for us to get married. We've never discussed the whens and hows. I'm assuming you'll want something small and tasteful. There must be a chapel at Saint Thomas's. We could have a noon wedding followed by a luncheon at the Plaza? Whatever it's going to be, we'd better make reservations. The week before Christmas will rush things, but I can take time off then and I assume you can, too. Thought maybe we'd go to Aruba or Saint John's. So what do you think?"

Meg was stunned into silence.

"You're speechless, my love." Rick laughed

aloud. "So drink up and then we'll order. Who ever heard of a speechless lawyer?"

The champagne was delicious. The menu was extensive. Meg had no appetite and tried to order a simple salad. When the waiter reappeared, Rick ordered poached salmon for himself. "My lady just wants a salad," he said. "Make it a lobster salad." He winked at Meg.

My lady? The words irritated her. Meg, who had smoked for a few months during her last year in high school and again during her first year in law school, suddenly longed for a cigarette. She wanted to run out of this lovely restaurant. Her body twitched. Her brain was a mass of conflicting, mostly irrelevant, emotions. *I love him, so why aren't I glowing with delight?*

"Say something, darling," Rick commanded.

She shook her head.

"You act as if you are in shock. Long engagements are not healthy, so let's get down to details."

She forced a laugh and flipped the pages of the little book to December. "I am a ninny, aren't I? So tell me, where are we going to live? How are we going to afford this tasteful bash at the Plaza and the honeymoon in the Caribbean?"

"You've been paying off your loan twice as fast as the bank requires. You can make single payments or perhaps no payments for a while. And then there's your bonus. Last year you said it was ten thousand dollars. I assume this year's will be similar, enough for a wedding dress and a luncheon reception."

His evaluation of *her* income and expenditures was irritating, but she said nothing.

"And I?" He bowed his head and crossed his hands across his chest. "I am Mr. J. Paul Moneybags. I am in the process of hitting it rich in the stock market. I have invested very cleverly. I've also received a ten-thousand-dollar raise. What do you think of that?"

"I think the raise is terrific. Congratulations." She lifted her glass to him.

The plates their waiter placed in front of them were artfully arranged; the popovers were warm and crisp.

"You were right, Rick," Meg said when she had taken a few bites. "I did want lobster. It's delicious. Thank you."

"Of course I was right. Now let's talk about apartments. I really want us to buy a co-op or condo. I'm sorry you didn't like the Fifth Avenue place, but if you want more space and light, I'm willing to look farther east in the sixties or seventies. Actually, I've seen several possibilities."

"My friend Amy owns a large apartment overlooking a garden in Jackson Heights," she said tentatively.

"Queens is out."

Just like that, he declared Queens beyond his consideration. "How much were these possibilities you went to see?" With some effort, she managed to speak sweetly at the same time that she was wondering when he had found time to apartment-hunt.

"Two to three hundred thousand."

"And the maintenance fee and the mortgage payments?"

"A couple of thousand a month. But let me tell

you about the apartment I saw on Sixty-sixth Street. Windows and views . . ."

While Rick described that apartment and two others, Meg forced herself to eat most of her salad and then she simply sat and looked down at her hands clasped tightly together in her lap.

At last Rick stopped talking. He placed his knife and fork across his plate and remained silent until the waiter had poured their coffee. Then he leaned across the table. "What is the matter with you, Meg? I planned this lunch to be memorable. I thought you were as anxious to marry me as I am to marry you."

Meg could say nothing.

Suddenly Rick grinned. "You want an engagement ring. Is that it? You said you didn't, but you do. Oh, darling, if you want a ring—"

"I do not want a ring, Rick." Meg spoke through her tightly clenched teeth.

"Then what do you want?" Rick's eyes blazed. "Tell me. What do you want?"

She tried to lift her coffee cup but it rattled in the saucer. He signaled the waiter for the check, gulped down his coffee, and hurried her out to the car. When they were both seated, he turned and asked her again what she wanted.

"I don't know," Meg said. "I think I still want to marry you—"

"You *think* you want to marry me?" He was incredulous. "You *think*—"

"But I'm beginning to wonder what it is I really do want. For years I've had one goal: to make it big in a big law firm in a big city. But I panic when you talk about *owning* an apartment in the city. Home, to me, is a house with grass and flowers. And ever since I met Alice—"

"Who?"

"The three-year-old in Stonefield who calls your brother Mr. Giraffe. I'm not sure I want to wait years to have a baby."

"The mommy track? I can't believe that. Not you, Meg. You've invested too much to earn a first-class law degree and a top-salary position in a prestigious firm. Four years from now, when you are a partner, if you *still* want a child, you might be able to juggle your time to accommodate *one* child along with your career. Certainly not now. In the meantime, I want us to be married."

She shook her head slowly and tried to order her thoughts. "I'm not ready to choose a date for a tasteful bash at the Plaza."

"I suppose you want a fried-chicken reception with dancing in the carport," he said with a sneer.

"Perhaps. I had fun at that wedding, Rick."

He turned on the engine and screeched out of the parking lot. Neither of them spoke until they were pulling into Miss Pearce's lane.

"I'm not a doormat, Meg. I won't hang around waiting for you to make up your mind. I assume we can put on a good front this evening. I'll leave first thing tomorrow morning. You'll have two weeks to decide. If you want to marry me, give me a call and I'll drive up and get you. Otherwise . . . ."

"I'm sorry, Rick."

"I am, too. I thought we were perfect together."

"You and the person you thought I was—and I thought I was—*were* perfect together. What's happening, whatever it is, is not your fault, Rick. It's mine."

When they had greeted Miss Pearce, Meg went upstairs where she hung two dresses and a skirt in the closet, splashed cold water on her face, and renewed her blusher and lipstick.

Then she crept down the stairs and out across the lawns to the secret garden. For a long time she sat on a wall. She was only vaguely aware of her surroundings. Her thoughts were random wisps that came from nowhere and led nowhere. *Sitting on a wall like Humpty Dumpty . . . great fall . . . couldn't put Humpty Dumpty together again . . .* Idly, she pulled grass out from a bed of plants that hugged the ground. She thought about the book that had inspired this garden. The secret garden had tamed bratty little Mary Lenox and healed a self-pitying, hysterical boy. The book and this garden had also comforted a little girl named Harriet Pearce.

Meg had once had a garden. She wanted to think that she would have one again in the future. A garden, and a baby. Did she also want Rick? She thought of the few other boys and men she had dated, none of them for more than a few months. All were gauche compared with Rick. She had certainly admired Rick, and enjoyed his company. Did she truly love him? That was the question.

She looked up and saw Piet looking down at her from the top of the ramp. She wondered how long he'd been there. She waved her hand but said nothing.

"Want to be alone?" he asked.

She nodded.

"Please pick four of the biggest, ripest tomatoes and bring them to the house when you come. I'll leave a basket for them here. Pick more if you want." He turned. "No hurry."

She rose and strolled among the beds, pulling a weed here and snapping off a dead flower there. Then she took the basket and began to pick the tomatoes. There were at least a dozen that were perfectly ripe. She bit into one. The flesh was warm and the juice dripped down her chin. With neither seasoning nor dressing it was delicious. She smiled and walked back to the house.

Miss Pearce and Rick were sitting outside near where Piet was tending charcoal.

"You've been gone a very long time," Rick said. His eyes widened. "Look at you."

"Good straight from the vine, aren't they?" Miss Pearce laughed.

"Delicious. I now know what they mean about the best watermelon being stolen watermelon. Forgive me for eating without asking. But how did you know?" She looked down and saw the evidence. Her white dress was splashed with tomato juice and seeds—and garden soil. "The dress is cotton but I guess I'd better soak the stains. Shall I put the tomatoes I didn't eat in the fridge?"

"Leave them on the counter, Meg, and in the future, don't apologize for eating or picking anything growing in my garden."

During drinks and dinner, Meg marveled at Rick's good humor. He was amusing as he talked about his work and his raise. He told Miss Pearce that he had seen Joe DiMaggio on Fifty-second

Street and went on to discuss stars of the current baseball season. Meg hadn't known that Rick was interested in sports.

Miss Pearce certainly was. "Television is one of the blessings of this age," she said, "especially for us old folks. My father used to take me to Fenway Park once or twice every season. Those were the only games I got to see. Now I can see several games a week and I don't have to climb up into bleachers to broil in the sun or shiver in the shade. And in the winter I can see movies and plays without leaving the warmth of my fireside. Some people may yearn for the good old days; I'm not one of them."

Piet prepared the dinner, which they ate outside: charcoal-broiled steaks, green beans, and pasta tossed with fresh basil and tomatoes. He said very little except to contribute the name of a player or a score.

When Meg and Piet returned from the kitchen with ice cream, cookies, and coffee, Rick was discussing apartments. "I have the down payment, or I will have when I sell some stocks that are turning out well for me. But Meg is a dyed-in-the-wool conservative as far as money is concerned. When I bring up the subject of apartments, all she can talk about is the mortgage and the carrying charges. You'd think I was suggesting we buy the Taj Mahal, instead of a modest three-room apartment in a decent neighborhood." Rick laughed at silly Meg. "If I just had a little more to put down, or if I knew what I could count on, so that I could reassure Meg, it would—"

"How about some coffee?" Meg said loudly, interrupting him in mid-sentence and blushing with shame. She would never have believed that Rick could be such a blatant beggar.

"And ice cream and cookies?" added Piet. "There's a game on this evening. Shall we watch?"

Rick took a bite out of a cookie and then turned back to Miss Pearce. "As I was saying—"

"Let's not talk about money and real estate. The night is too beautiful." Meg asked the only question she could think of. "How do you keep the bugs away, Miss Pearce?"

"With that lantern thing over there." She spoke absently. "You want to know where you stand, Frederick? I'll tell you."

"I'll just take my coffee down to the secret garden," Meg said. She couldn't silence Rick but she refused to be his accomplice. Years ago Meg Bower had promised herself that once she was out of school, she would never, never ask anyone for a favor.

"May I join you?" Piet asked.

"Stay here, both of you," Miss Pearce commanded. "What I have to say concerns all three of you. None of this will be news to Piet, of course. To put it bluntly, Fred, my death will not benefit you in any way. My father loved you. You were such a charming little boy—big boy, too." Miss Pearce chuckled. "Your education is your inheritance from my father, and from me."

"And Piet?" Rick asked.

"The arboretum is tied up with a land conservancy so that it can never be built upon and will remain more or less as it is now—at least that is my hope. There isn't much money left and most of that is in a trust to maintain the arboretum. Everything else goes to Piet."

Rick turned and glared at his brother, who said nothing.

"Before you say something you will regret, Frederick, remember that Piet could have had an education equal to yours. Instead he elected to stay here to help your father, who was not well enough to continue caring for all of this." With a sweep of her arm, she indicated her entire acreage.

"After your father died, Piet stayed on. He loves these gardens as much as I do. We are not demonstrative, but I hope that Piet knows that he has been the son I never had. That's all I have to say. I'm going to bed, to finish the mystery I'm reading. Have to find out who done it."

She held out her hands to Piet, who took them and pulled her to her feet. She patted his cheek and then she turned to Rick. "Try to understand," she said. She smiled at Meg. "I'm looking forward to these two weeks with you, girl. Thank you for coming."

"I thank you," Meg said.

As soon as the old lady was in the house, Rick leaped to his feet. "Sneaky Piet," he shouted. "Of all the underhanded . . . You're the lawyer, Meg. What do you think?"

Meg said nothing for a moment and then she spoke cautiously. "I can see that you are disappointed, Rick, but I know that you are grateful for your very fine—and very expensive—education. It's what you wanted, what you can use."

"And Piet gets the house and the land and . . . everything else."

"The house is lovely but it's not a mansion," Piet said. "It will come to me with about twenty acres—no gold mines or oil wells—and an old Mercedes. These are things I will treasure. Do they mean anything to you, Fred?" Piet stacked the cups and plates on a tray. "You got what you treasure, an education."

"I deserved a fine education. You couldn't have been accepted at a good school."

"True. I think I may be mildly dyslexic."

"But you read." Meg was bewildered. "Your house is full of books."

"Yes, I like to read now. It took me a long time to learn. When I was in third grade and Fred was in first, he could read better than I. I believed the people who said I was stupid."

"Poor little brother," Rick jeered. "Your story breaks my heart." He jumped to his feet. "When I said I'd be leaving first thing in the morning, I misspoke. I'm leaving now, tonight. In the meantime, brother, you can just go on chauffeuring her car, and cooking her meals and mucking in her garden."

"Good night, Fred," Piet said and picked up the tray and went inside.

"I'm sorry, Rick," Meg whispered as she followed him to the car. "You meant for this to be a very special day. I'm sorry it had to end this way. Be angry with me, for presenting myself as someone as ambitious and sophisticated as you. I thought I was your kind of person. I still may be; I just don't know. But please don't be angry with Piet. He's not guilty of anything except loving Miss Pearce and this land."

"You're on his side?"

"No, Rick, I'm not. I just want you to accept what I think is a fact. People like us, who are very ambitious, sacrifice some of the gentler aspects of our personalities. You needed a fine education to get ahead. And you got it. You'd like to have more of her money but you don't want what she values—her land and her house. Do you doubt that Piet will cherish them?"

Rick laughed without humor. "Don't you begin to cherish Piet, Meg. This back-to-nature pose doesn't suit you." He opened the car door.

Meg laid her hand on his arm. "Don't drive back to the city tonight, Rick. Please. You're tired and upset. If you don't feel you can sleep under Piet's roof, then go to a motel."

He brushed her aside and climbed into the car. "If you come to your senses in the next two weeks, let me know. I *may* drive up to get you." He drove off in a swirl of gravel.

Meg walked back to the lawn area where Piet placed a glass of iced tea into her hand. "Thanks, Piet. Don't feel bad about what happened this evening. It's my fault. I had upset Rick before we ever got here. He wanted to set a wedding date and I—" She shook her head.

"You don't want to?"

"I can't. Rick and I thought we were two of a kind, ambitious, hard-working . . . Now I'm not so sure about me."

"He would have to know about Miss Pearce's will sometime, but I'm sorry it had to come on this day.

Losing you, or the fear of losing you, would be . . . Poor Fred."

"I begged him not to drive back to the city while he was upset, but I doubt he was listening. Thank you for the tea, Piet." She held out her hand to him. "Thanks too for the dinner. Those steaks were superb." She turned and then stopped. "I'm afraid your brother doesn't fully appreciate you, Piet. I hope you can forgive him."

"Do you have a brother?" he asked. She nodded. "And do you fully appreciate him?"

She was stunned by the question. "I was very proud of him when I was a little girl; he was such a fine athlete, at least by Brinton standards."

"And as an adult are you proud of him?"

"I don't know. I don't see him often. My fault. No Piet, I don't suppose I do appreciate my brother."

Piet grinned. "That's the way it is with siblings, though I do find much to admire in Fred."

"What?"

"His confidence and daring. I would never have been able to ask Miss Pearce how much money she intended to leave me; I have trouble presenting bills for the work I do. I envy his education and polish. The way people look at him when he enters a room. The way he knows what to say on any occasion. And today, while you were down in the garden, he told us that he had just received a ten-thousand-dollar raise. That's two hundred dollars a week more than he's already receiving. I know people who *live* on less than his raise. It boggles my mind." He turned toward the path to his house. "Good night, Meg," he called over his shoulder.

Chapter Ten

As soon as she awoke, Meg began to worry about Rick. He should not have driven back to the city late at night when he was both tired and angry.

"Piet's worried about Rick," Miss Pearce said when they met in the garden. "And so am I. How early can you call him?"

"Ten?" Meg said. "But perhaps Piet—"

"Piet's off hobnobbing with a nursery pal. He'll be gone all day."

It had not rained during the week, so Meg watered individual plants. When she dialed Rick's number, she received no answer. There was still no answer at noon.

"He rented the car for the weekend so he's probably driven to the beach. He has a number of friends out in the Hamptons. What about the *Times*?"

"Should have asked a neighbor to bring mine by. Piet left before the store opened. Do you drive? You could take the car . . ."

"I have a license, but I haven't driven for a very long time. How far is it? About a mile? I'll walk. Can't be much farther than from Macy's to Bloomingdale's."

"Macy's to Bloomingdale's is flat. Here to Stonefield is downhill—easy. Coming back is not."

It was, as Miss Pearce had said, an easy walk into town, and pleasant. Through breaks in the dense hedgerow on her left she occasionally glimpsed the lush valley dotted with fields, ponds, and small forests. On her right, houses were tucked into the woods. One was a shanty, a hunting shack perhaps. Another was an authentic Colonial surrounded by velvety lawns and clipped evergreens. She walked past a rustic modern house, a new log cabin, and three small houses of no distinction except that they looked comfortable and well cared-for.

There were sidewalks in Stonefield, beginning at the church and extending the few blocks through town. Meg paused to admire a Federal-style house set close to the walk and then went on to the shops. She stepped into the gallery where the pretty pregnant woman named Emily greeted her like an old friend.

"It was nice to meet Piet's brother," she said. "They look a lot alike, don't they?"

"They are both blonds with blue eyes, but they are *very* different. Rick's a city boy."

"Country mouse, city mouse. I lived in Boston all my life until two years ago. Now you couldn't get me to move back for all the tea in the Boston harbor. I even like the winters here. Piet, or one of his men, plows our lane. He can do almost anything—design landscapes, make things grow . . . And yet he's so—I hate the word 'sensitive'—but he's kind and well read. Keith and I are very fond of Piet." Emily giggled. "So is everybody else in town. There's some mystery about a broken engagement—I gather that the cake had already been baked when the wedding was called off—but no one will discuss it with newcomers like Keith and me. His brother's probably told you all about it."

Meg shook her head. "Rick just said that it happened two days before the wedding—many years ago, I think."

"I think so, too. It's time for him to find a wife. That's what I tell him. Last summer a terrific young woman rented one of our rooms for a month. Piet was putting in lawn for us and she thought he was really something. He wouldn't even look at her. His reason? She was writing her master's thesis. What's that got to do with anything? you ask. I can't imagine."

"I can't, either. He's so gentle and yet . . ."

"He's got a temper, let me tell you. You should have seen him take out after a boy he caught throwing rocks at the beavers. Piet grabbed the kid under the arms and lifted him so that his toes just barely touched the ground while he delivered a lecture that would raise blisters on a stone."

A potential customer came in and asked about Hudson River paintings. Emily pulled out a huge oil of pastel mountains, waterfall, and rocky stream. A man with a sleek dog at his side looked down adoringly at an insipid woman in a white dress with a white bird perched on her finger. The frame was a garish mixture of black and gold. The shopper studied the painting, his hands clasped in front of his chest as if in prayer.

"The artist?" he asked.

"We don't know. It's not signed. We can't even date it accurately . . ."

Meg walked around the gallery and then stopped in front of a primitive of a little girl with a kitten in her lap. She was dark, like Alice.

"Do you like it?" Emily called to her.

"I do. I don't know enough about art to say why, but I'd like to hug that child."

Meg said good-bye to Emily and walked among the tables in the open market. Then she bought the *Times* and an ice-cream cone, and headed back. She was sweaty and panting when she flopped down under a maple in Miss Pearce's garden.

Rick did not answer his phone late in the afternoon, and Meg's worry increased. *If he'd been in an accident, who would be informed? His nearest relative? That was Piet and he wasn't home, either.*

She finally reached Rick at ten. "Just wanted to be sure you were okay," she said, trying to sound casual. "Did you do something fun today?"

"You've relinquished your right to question me, Meg." He hung up.

Miss Pearce had gone to her bedroom, but Meg knocked on her door and entered a large room with ornate moldings and mantel. The old lady looked small in a huge four-poster bed. When Meg had reported on Rick, Miss Pearce phoned Piet to pass the message along. She asked Piet if he'd have time on Monday for the arboretum and was silent while Piet spoke. Then she laughed. "I could be ready by six. You know that. But my guest?" She looked a question at Meg.

Six o'clock in the morning? Meg was stunned. "Whenever you say."

"Think we'll let our city girl sleep in tomorrow. We'll be ready by seven-thirty." She chuckled at something he said and hung up.

"I like this room, Miss Pearce."

"I, too. My great-grandfather had this bed made before anyone ever thought of queen- and king-sized beds. We put in a full bathroom downstairs when climbing the steps became difficult for my father. Then we moved the bed. After my father died I decided that I had no need of a formal parlor, so this room became my bedroom." She patted the mattress as if it were an old friend. "I was conceived in this bed. If God is kind, I will die in it."

Miss Pearce was waiting in her golf cart when Piet drove up the lane at exactly 7:30 the next morning. She waved to him and then set off across the lawn. Meg climbed into the truck and the two-vehicle caravan crept toward the back of the garden and a hedge of mostly mature evergreens.

"I had no idea there were so many variations on the color green." Meg laughed with delight. "They blend together like a tapestry. Did God design that hedge or did you?"

"It was a joint effort. God—or birds—planted some of the pines, hemlocks, and green spruces. Dad put in the blue spruces and firs, and the yellow chamys. Miss Pearce and I added the dwarf conifers in the foreground."

"Is this part of the arboretum, Piet?"

"No, but all of these species are included in the arboretum."

Miss Pearce stopped her cart in the middle of a wooden plank bridge over a deep gully. While she sat studying the portal on the opposite bank, Meg studied it, too. Two tall bare tree trunks rose like pillars on either side of the path just beyond the end of the bridge. A branch from one tree was partially broken and the end of it was hung up in the opposite tree on an angle. A carved wooden sign hung from the cross branch on chains of unequal lengths so that the sign was straight. "Catherine Pearce Memorial Arboretum" it read. Acorns, pinecones, and maple wings had been carved around the words to form a border. Miss Pearce turned in her cart and threw a kiss to Piet.

"Tell me about the gateway and the sign, Piet," Meg asked.

"Just another case of God and me working together. God sent us a sixteen-inch snow early in October of eighty-seven, before the trees had begun to drop their leaves. Trees and branches crashed down all over the area. We had no power for more than a week. Those two locusts remained standing, so I cut all of the broken branches away except the one the sign hangs from."

"Tell me about the sign."

"Catherine was her mother. I gave her the new sign for Christmas but I didn't get it up until last week."

"Who carved it, Piet?"

"I did. Do you like it?"

"I think it's magnificent." She spoke truthfully.

Once they had crossed the bridge, they drove uphill along a bumpy path just wide enough for the truck. Ahead, Miss Pearce looked as if she could be thrown from the seat of the golf cart at any moment.

"Is she safe?" Meg asked.

"Not very, but she can go closer to the trees in her cart than I can drive her in the truck—and she feels independent. Feet are the only means of transportation up here except when it has been dry for a long spell. She hasn't been up since last October."

"But you walk up?"

"On cross-country skis in the winter. I wish you could see it then. In the spring I slosh up in rubber boots." He stopped the truck and jumped down. "We'll begin here."

That morning and every morning that week, Miss Pearce worked on an inventory of trees and shrubs, producing brass identifying tags for some and making lists of the tags still to be ordered. Piet lopped or sawed away dead branches and saplings growing too close to their mothers. He and Meg clipped and dug invasive plants away from prize plants. Several afternoons Piet and Meg returned to the arboretum after lunch.

For Meg, it was an educational experience. She learned that not all willows are weeping willows or even pussy willows, that not all birches have white bark and grow in clumps. Her education continued evenings when she and Miss Pearce talked about what they had seen during the day.

Miss Pearce told her that the real value of the arboretum, as she saw it, was their attempt to extend the range of certain desirable trees. They had planted many specimens that were not expected to live in the harsh Berkshire climate where winter temperatures could drop to 20 below zero. Most of these had died, but a few had been thriving for more than thirty-five years.

"It's important to extend the variety of trees in any locale," Miss Pearce said. "We never know which old favorites will be felled by disease or blight so we must have plenty of other trees to replace those that are lost."

"Elms," Meg said, to indicate that she understood.

"Before that it was the American chestnut. When Longfellow wrote, 'Under the spreading chestnut tree, the village smithy stands,' he was writing about a common tree. Now there are only a few. Scientists have been working for generations to try to produce a disease-resistant American chestnut. We have one that I first noticed in 1977. It's growing and it's healthy—so far." Miss Pearce rapped her knuckles on a wooden table and then crossed her fingers.

The old lady sighed. "Now some maples and pines may be threatened. But we keep introducing and testing trees and species. That's why nurserymen and dendrologists are interested in our project." She smiled and remained silent for a moment. "It gives me pleasure to know that I will be leaving something of value to the world—or at least to the area. Grandiose, aren't I?"

Meg shook her head. "I imagine that most people would like to contribute to the general good." She wondered if women saw their children as possible gifts to the world. And Meg's contribution? Nothing, so far.

One evening, after they had been poring over a lavishly illustrated book on Japanese maple trees, Miss Pearce put her hand over Meg's. "You know, my dear, I feel blessed because I know that the arboretum will be maintained for at least as long as Piet lives. You must understand, Meg, that there is no way I can divide this property with Frederick. He cares nothing about it. You do, however, and as Fred's wife—"

"I don't know that I will ever be his wife."

The old lady stared at Meg. "I thought—"

"We were engaged but I . . . I have a lot of thinking to do. He's wonderful, everything I thought I wanted in a husband. Once a year my firm has a big party. I've gone alone in previous years and been miserable. The truth is that I often feel uncomfortable in social situations. I was even nervous about coming up here in June." Meg laughed at herself, remembering. "This year, Rick went with me to the office party and I had a wonderful time. He has this remarkable talent for saying just the right thing. The problem is not Rick, but me." She turned away, picked up her book, and headed for the stairs. "I think I'll read in bed tonight . . ."

"Good idea, dear. I suspected that something was plaguing you. Thank you for telling me."

"It's not Rick's fault. You must believe that."

"Of course. Good night. You are a remarkable young woman, Meg. If I had a daughter . . . But I didn't."

Meg returned and planted a kiss on the woman's wrinkled cheek.

Chapter Eleven

As they were returning from the arboretum Friday noon, Piet said that Miss Pearce had suggested that they take the afternoon off. "She said you were intrigued with the Hudson River school of painting. We thought maybe you'd like to drive down to Olana, Frederic Church's home on the Hudson."

"I've never heard of Frederic Church. I don't think I ever heard of the Hudson River school until Sunday. Frankly, I thought the painting in the Stonefield gallery was insipid but I know practically nothing about art."

"Neither do I, but that shouldn't stop us from forming opinions."

"Definitely not." Meg laughed. "Some of the most ignorant people I know have the strongest opinions."

"Right. And then we'll have dinner and pontificate to one another on the merits of the Hudson River school."

"Comparing it to other art forms about which we know nothing."

He went off toward his A-frame, whistling. As she had on several previous occasions, Meg caught herself admiring the breadth of his back, the slimness of his hips, and the ease with which he moved. *Perhaps I should have declined the invitation,* she said to herself, and then she laughed at her own silliness. *I don't need to get me to a nunnery just because I notice broad shoulders.*

Upstairs, Meg took a yellow linen dress from the closet—and put it back. The dress would add weight to an occasion of no importance to either Piet or herself. It would also look inappropriate in a rusty pickup. She pulled a navy polo-shirt-grown-to-dress-length over her head and cinched it with a white straw belt, slipped her bare feet into flat-heeled sandals, and clipped the enamel earrings she had bought at the open-air market onto her lobes.

Piet arrived on foot and escorted her to the Mercedes. "Miss Pearce insists," he said.

"I'd give it to him, if he'd take it," she called after them. "Have a good time."

When they were through Stonefield, Meg turned to Piet and asked a question that had been on her mind for a long time. "Why do you call her Miss Pearce? She said that she thinks of you as her son. You obviously care for her. Why don't you call her Aunt Harriet or just Harriet?"

"She's asked me to call her Harriet, but I began life calling her Miss Pearce. She was our father's employer and she is mine. She pays me a generous salary which we never discuss. She is also fifty years older than I. So I call her what I was taught to call her when I learned to talk. Anything else sounds disrespectful or overly familiar."

"But Rick . . ."

"Freddy is different. He hasn't worked for her since he went off to college and he's well educated, more her equal. You heard from Fred? I thought he might come up this weekend."

"No. He hasn't called. I didn't expect him to."

The road led across the thruway into New York State, where the hills became lower and sparser until the land was almost flat. They passed through tiny villages, past fields and forests and then orchards. The first real town was Hudson, on the banks of the Hudson. Piet said it was an old whaling town. He drove down side streets to show her some architectural gems, many of which were clustered near the county courthouse.

They left the town on a road heading south along the river until a sign pointed the way up a narrow road to Olana. The road rose so that, looking back, Meg could still see the river. And then the house came into view!

She covered her mouth with her hand to stifle a laugh, hoping that Piet wouldn't notice.

"Terrific." Piet whooped. "Nineteenth-century fantasyland!"

"You've never been here?"

"Nope. The pictures don't do it justice." He drove into the parking lot, ran around the car to open the door for her, took her hand and hurried her toward the stone structure, which at first glimpse had made her think of a castle. It had many towers of varying sizes and shapes, all decorated with colorful tiles. Every window and doorway was surrounded by tiles in different patterns.

When the tour began, they were told that Frederic Church, one of the most popular artists of his day, had traveled in the East in 1867 and had returned to build a house that reflected Islamic art and architecture—mixed with Victorian clutter. The walls of the downstairs rooms were lavishly stenciled and hung with pictures by Church himself as well as by others, several on every wall. The doors were ornately carved and painted. Every table was crowded with books and objects. Oriental rugs were scattered over the floors. A stuffed peacock stood at the foot of the stairway.

In spite of the clutter, there was an amazing lightness about the house. The windows were large and had been designed to frame views of the river and the Catskill Mountains beyond. Meg found herself smiling ever more broadly as the guide pointed out the details of each room and told them about Mr. Church and his family and friends.

When they had been ushered from the house, Meg put her hand on Piet's arm. "What fun," she exclaimed.

He covered her hand with his and smiled down into her eyes and then drew away quickly. They walked around the grounds, which Mr. Church had also designed but which the state had neglected.

Piet drove several miles along the Hudson River to an unpretentious restaurant set back from the highway just enough to accommodate a parking lot. It would have looked grim except for the huge hanging baskets jammed with a colorful assortment of flowers.

"I've never been here, but Jerry says it's good," Piet said as he led her to the desk. They followed the host through a dark bar and then into a mostly glass room with a view of a wide lawn, train tracks, the Hudson River, and the Catskills.

"This is lovely, Piet," she said when they had been seated.

"Didn't look too promising until we got to this room. Do you want a drink or shall we order a bottle of wine?"

"Wine," she said and they studied the menu and decided to order fish.

When the waiter had poured their white wine and taken their orders, Piet asked Meg how she felt about the Hudson River school now.

She thought a moment.

"Don't think you have to be tactful," he said hastily. "I didn't paint the pictures."

"Okay, I'll tell you. In many cases I liked the frames better than the paintings. Mr. Church designed some beautifully carved frames, didn't he? I guess heavy romantic landscapes just aren't my thing."

"And the house?"

"I loved it. It was so personal. I think I'd like Mr. Church, were we to meet. Not that I could stand to live with all that clutter. But I don't have to. He did and he liked it. What do you think?"

"You've said it all. I'm glad to have seen it, and a little of that stencil work and carving and painting would have been great. Living with so much of it, you'd always feel like the hour after Thanksgiving dinner—stuffed. Wish I could get my hands on the grounds—and had the staff and the money to do it properly."

"How'd you like his collection of fake old masters in the dining room?"

"I couldn't figure that out. He told everyone they were fakes, so he wasn't trying to pass them off as anything but what they were. But why would he want fake anything?"

Meg laughed. "Do share with me your view on plastic flowers."

"I don't have to. You know how I feel about plastic flowers without asking. Silk flowers, too. Actually silk flowers are worse than plastic ones because they look so real." He put his hand over hers. "But I like dried flowers."

Meg looked into his eyes—and away, and scooted her hand from under his. "What kinds of paintings do you like?" she asked.

"I told you, I don't know much about art. I've been told that I should love Picasso, but I don't. That's not quite true; I've seen a few Picassos that I like. I like Van Gogh and Monet and Renoir. And you? What do you like?"

When the salad had been served, she spoke. "I'd planned to find out when I got to New York. Spend time in museums and galleries. I haven't done much looking yet. But last Sunday at the Stonefield gallery—when I saw the Hudson River painting—I also saw a primitive of a little girl. She looked like Alice and I wanted to hug her. And I have a wonderful walrus that I can't quite describe to you. It's a wood carving and as smooth as velvet with interesting designs in the wood. He's lying on his back and I rub his tummy every time I—" Suddenly she stopped and stared at Piet. "You know my walrus," she breathed. "You carved him. You gave him to your brother and he . . . Oh dear, Piet. You gave him to Rick. I'll. . . ."

"You'll keep him. I'd have carved him for you, Meg, if I'd known you then. I'm glad you like him."

"I love him, Piet. He comforts me." They looked at one another in silence until Meg was aware of inappropriate vibrations filling the space between them. She looked down at her plate. "Tell me about your carving, Piet. What other things do you make? Do you sell them?"

The waiter brought their dinners and they ate in silence and then Piet began to speak. "I carve in the winter and I sell some of my things at the Stonefield gallery."

"I didn't see any."

"Because there aren't any. I worked on the sign for Miss Pearce this year. That took most of the winter. The three other pieces I did were sold two weeks after the gallery opened for the season."

"And next winter?"

"Nika, who owns the gallery, and Emily want me to do a few major pieces and as many small ones as possible."

"Will you enjoy that?"

He grinned broadly. "Oh yes! I've already bought a bunch of books on tape. What I do . . . Are you sure you're interested?" When she nodded, he continued. "I set my alarm for five A.M. so that if it has snowed during the night, I can plow out my customers who have to get to work. If it hasn't snowed, I build up the fire in my stove and go back to bed and read for a while. After breakfast I phone Miss Pearce to be sure she's okay. Then I tend my plants. I carve while I listen to music or a taped book. Late in the morning I walk to town for the mail and paper and then back to Miss Pearce's. I usually stay for lunch. In the afternoon I carve and listen until time for the evening news. If conditions are right, I sometimes ski for a couple of hours in the afternoon."

"Cross-country or downhill?"

"Sometimes one, sometimes the other. I also go to Holland to visit my mother during the winter. Last year I went on to Rome and Naples."

"It sounds like a good life, Piet. Tell me about the plants you tend in the winter."

"I've made a sort of portable scaffolding that goes in front of the window wall in my living room. I fill it with cuttings and seeds that need an early start. One day I'll have a real greenhouse. I also spend a lot of time studying catalogs and making plans for my clients. Now you tell me about you."

The waiter cleared their plates and brought coffee. Meg told him about her apartment and her job.

"You don't sound very enthusiastic about your job."

"It's better now than it was. Mergers and acquisitions bored me. So much detail. Now I'm in trusts and have been writing wills. That's okay but I'll be on to something else when I get back after my vacation."

"I hope you'll like it."

"I have to like it, or at least tolerate it. Let's talk

about something else, Piet. Those mountains on the other side of the river, for example."

"The Catskills, home of Rip Van Winkle."

She turned from the window to look into his eyes. Bolts of something Meg did not wish to define flew back and forth between them! They stared at one another until she forced herself to look out of the window again and he signaled the waiter for more coffee and the check.

"Let's go Dutch," she said and then laughed. "Perhaps that is not the phrase to use with a Dutchman."

"I don't mind the words but I won't accept the concept, Meg. If you don't shut your purse, I'll be insulted."

She obeyed. "Thank you. It was a very good dinner."

He looked thoughtful for a moment. "Was it?" he asked. "I can't remember. I had swordfish, didn't I? And a baked potato?"

She couldn't remember, either. He must have had swordfish. What had she had? Shrimp. With rice? "It was delicious." She spoke positively to hide her confusion.

They talked about the garden on the way home. He asked her if she'd like to go to the Tanglewood rehearsal in the morning and told her who would be doing what.

She should not go alone with Rick's brother. Alone? There would be thousands of people and it would be broad daylight. "Thank you. I'll be ready at nine. Or should we go earlier?"

"Quarter to nine." He drove the car into the garage, jumped out and opened the door for Meg and escorted her to the door. His hand burned her elbow. "I've enjoyed this day, Meg. Thank you." He turned and loped toward the path.

What would it be like to be kissed by Piet? She dismissed the question as soon as it popped into her head. She'd only asked the question because Piet's mouth was shaped so differently from Rick's. It was fuller, and some might say more sensuous. But she certainly had no romantic feelings toward him. He was her fiancé's—more accurately, her former fiancé's—brother. They'd had a pleasant afternoon together. That was all.

The next morning, they met as mere acquaintances. They chatted sporadically about the weather and the program, much as one chats with a stranger on a bus, neither giving anything of himself. She paid for her own ticket. They found excellent seats in the Tanglewood shed and sat as if there were a glass wall between them, so that their shoulders never touched. At the end of the first half, he suggested coffee but he did not take her elbow as they walked to the back of the shed and out onto the lawn.

As they walked along a crowded path, Meg turned and there, almost at her side, was Jocelyn Montgomery.

The girl smiled brightly. "It's Rick's brother, Peter de Graaf. How nice to see you again. And ah . . ."

"Meg Bower," Piet said quickly. "My name, incidentally, is Piet Graaf. Fred, as I call him, added the 'de.' "

"Fred. Rick. Either is a nice name. And 'de

Graaf is certainly distinguished-sounding. Isn't it a pity he didn't come with me this morning? I left him by the pool with some boring old papers he said he had to study." She pouted prettily. "Maybe the four of us could go out to dinner together. Wouldn't that be fun?"

Simply hilarious! Meg thought. "He comes up every weekend?"

Jocelyn rested her chin on her finger. "He's been up every weekend since the middle of July. Shall we plan on dinner together next weekend?"

"Let's leave it to Fred. He knows where to find his brother." She took Piet's arm and they pushed on through the crowd.

By the time they had arrived at the food tables, Meg's brain and emotions were overloaded. Rick had been in the Berkshires when he had said he was in Chicago. That fact . . . Was it a fact? Perhaps Jocelyn lied or made a mistake. Meg was confused.

She was also remorseful; she'd put Piet in an awkward position. She should have spoken up immediately and said that she was not Piet's girlfriend, that she had, in fact, been engaged to marry Piet's brother. Miss Ringlets should have known that. Rick said he had told her. Had he?

"My brother is a fool," Piet muttered.

"He's just trying to get her father to transfer the Webster account to his agency. At least that's how the whole thing started." Why was she defending Rick?

After the concert, they walked to the car in silence. During the drive back to Miss Pearce's, she tried to talk about the performance. He said nothing until he had stopped the car in front of the garage.

"You're hurting, Meg."

"No I'm not. I'm not hurting; I'm mad. And not just at Rick. I'm mad at myself. I should have told Curlylocks that you and I are not a pair. I apologize, Piet."

"No need. I'd like . . ." He did not look at her but kept his eyes fixed on the steering wheel. "I have a friend who has a swimming pond. We could have a fast-food sandwich and then . . . But perhaps—"

"Terrific. I'd love to go swimming today. Cool off my hot head."

"Good," he breathed, turning to grin at her. "I don't quite know . . . Should I apologize for my brother?"

"No, you should not. I'd rather we didn't mention him again, Piet. I can't bad-mouth him to you because you are his brother. And right now I can't think of anything either pleasant or neutral to say about him. So let's forget him and go have a good time."

When they had both picked up their swim suits and towels, they drove to a chain eatery on the highway. Meg told Piet about the will she had written for the man she called Mr. X. Although he was a Wall Street bigwig, he would not be recognized beyond New York City except, possibly, in the financial community. She told about the many wives, and children and stepchildren and grandchildren and stepgrandchildren.

"What a good argument for monogamy." Piet laughed. He told her about an old Stonefield woman who had willed her house and all the money she had, a few thousand dollars, to a white Angora cat and his progeny. "When she died, the executor, the local banker, found a young couple to live in the house rent free in exchange for caring for Fluffy. Everyone was happy until . . ."—he paused dramatically and then went on—"a local wag whose cat had kittens, some of whom were white, announced that Fluffy had sired them. He took the kittens to the young couple. Others did the same. By the end of the year, Fluffy was blamed for something like forty kittens. The young couple moved out. The executor hired a woman to take care of the cats. Fluffy died the next year but still litters of kittens were dropped off by people who claimed they were Fluffy's grandchildren. Who could prove they were not?"

"So what happened?"

"The banker eventually sold the house and gave the money, and all the cats and kittens they could catch, to the local animal shelter. In the meantime, it gave the people in town something to talk about. Some people thought all cats should be drowned. Other suggested asking the Ford Foundation to build a cat hotel on the old lady's property."

"Did a lawyer write the old lady's will or did she do it herself?" Meg asked as they walked across the parking lot to the car.

"A lawyer in Lenox who retired to Florida soon after the old lady died."

"He was negligent, you know. He should have dissuaded her from the 'progeny' part. That's what lawyers are for."

* * *

Piet turned off the highway into a long driveway that led to a small white house. "When I called my friend, he said that he and his wife and the kids had to go meet some long-lost relatives but that we were to make ourselves at home. You can change in the garage."

The pond was large and clear, reflecting the green grass and wild flowers that surrounded it. Meg ran out of the garage humming, "By the sea, by the sea, by the beautiful sea." Piet ran up on the dock after her, singing, "By the pond, by the pond." *His voice is worse than mine*, Meg thought as she dived into the water and came up shivering and laughing.

"I should have warned you that it is spring-fed and always cold." Piet swam along beside her, across the pond and back, across and back.

Meg raised her hand to splash him and then lowered it gently into the water. If she splashed him, he would splash her and she would splash him and he would grab her. And then . . . She continued to swim sedately from one side to the other, grateful for the cold water that was keeping erotic thoughts under control.

When she was tired, she went quickly from the dock to the shore and wrapped a huge towel around herself before she dropped onto a chaise and closed her eyes.

He swam a few more laps and then came ashore and dropped down on a straw mat on the grass near her chair.

"You're a good swimmer, Piet," she said without opening her eyes.

"So are you, Meg. And you look terrific in a bathing suit. Sorry. I shouldn't notice such things about my brother's girl, should I?"

"I'm not his girl. Not now."

Neither of them said anything for a long time. Meg savored the warmth of the sun on her body. If it were not for Piet's electric presence, she might have relaxed.

"My father had a proverb he repeated over and over, every time Fred and I had a fight," he murmured.

"Was that often?"

"Very. Seems to be normal for kids when they are eight, ten, twelve years old. It also seems to drive parents batty. Parents think children should love each other."

"True. I never fought with my brother. Guess he was too much older. What was the proverb?"

"Proverbs, chapter eighteen, verse nine: 'A brother offended is harder to be won than a strong city; and their contentions are like the bars of a castle.' " Piet rose to his feet and lifted his eyes to the sky. "Did you have to remind me of that, Pop?" He laughed without humor. "Let's go home, Meg. Go get dressed."

Meg obeyed and they drove back to Stonefield in silence. They had begun the day as polite acquaintances; they ended it the same way. In between, for a few hours, and yesterday too, they had been familiar companions. Polite was proper; familiar was not.

Chapter Twelve

SUNDAY it was too muggy to work in the garden after ten A.M. Piet picked up the *Times* and left it just inside Miss Pearce's door.

"I wonder why he didn't come in," Miss Pearce said. Then she peered closely at Meg and said nothing more.

It was a lovely quiet day, the kind of day Meg liked best. Miss Pearce watched two baseball games. Meg read the *Times* thoroughly, and worked the puzzle. After dinner she opened a mystery by Josephine Tey that Miss Pearce recommended. She read late into the night. Every time her mind wandered, she yanked it back to the book.

Monday was even hotter and more humid than it had been the previous day. Driving to the arboretum beside Piet, she tried to make conversation. Piet said almost nothing. They worked side by side in silence, and Meg was glad when it was time to go back to the house for lunch. Piet did not suggest that they return to the arboretum in the afternoon. He declined Miss Pearce's invitation to dinner.

Tuesday and Wednesday were days like Monday except that the atmosphere and the silence were even more oppressive.

Thursday Miss Pearce announced that she was not going to the arboretum and advised Piet and Meg not to go, either. "You did listen to the weather report, didn't you, Piet?"

"Yes, but it was too indefinite to mean anything. Rain beginning sometime around noon. *Could* be heavy. *Could* be accompanied by thunder. If it starts to rain, I'll hop in my truck and hurry home. I agree that you should stay here."

"It's impossible for me to make a quick getaway in my cart." The old lady laughed. "And the top is neither wind- nor rainproof."

"And you've finished your inventory," Meg added. "Piet said we could complete our work in another couple of hours. So let's get to it. It might be too muddy tomorrow and I'd hate to leave a job unfinished."

"I like your spirit, Meg, but if it begins to sprinkle, you make Piet bring you home."

Meg agreed. Piet drove to the end of the path where they left the truck and walked deep into mature woods, carrying their tools. The ground between tall evergreens was covered with a cushion of needles so that there were few weeds and no grass, just young evergreens and fern.

"Doesn't look like there's much to be—" Meg stopped speaking as she saw Piet pull a wild grapevine out of a pine. They clipped the vines close to the ground and pulled them away from the trees. It was heavy work but they kept at it as clouds began to gather above them.

"Just that one hemlock left," Piet said, looking up at the sky. "But I think—"

"Don't say it. We promised we'd go home when it began to sprinkle. I haven't felt a single drop." She ran off to the hemlock and began pulling on the vine that rose from the ground on twisted ropes almost two inches in diameter. Tentacles clung to the needles of the tree. She pulled while Piet sawed the main stem and then clipped the young vines growing up around it.

"Sorry, Mrs. Hemlock," Piet called while he continued to saw. "I guess I haven't been off in this far corner for a couple of years. I didn't know you were about to be choked to death. I don't think you could have made it another year."

"Poor Mrs. Hemlock," Meg sympathized.

They worked frantically as the sky continued to darken. It was almost black when they picked up their tools and headed back toward the truck. Wind began to blow; the first drops fell. They ran but the storm was gathering faster than Meg could have imagined possible. Lightning flashed in the distance and then closer. Thunder seemed to be rolling toward them. The wind intensified.

Piet grabbed the clippers Meg was carrying and threw them under a spruce with his saw and loppers. Then he took her hand and ran, with strength and speed, uphill, away from where the truck was parked. Branches whipped her arms. Her shirt was soaked through. Her sneakers were weighted with mud. Water ran in rivers down her face. Still they ran on. When she thought she could never catch another breath, Piet stopped and held pine branches aside with one arm while he guided her to a door that opened into a small shed.

With the door closed behind them, the space was lit only by slashes of gray light creeping between slits in the siding. Their raspy breaths were punctuated by a clap of thunder that seemed to be directly overhead. They faced one another, their shoulders heaving in unison, water running down their faces and necks. Meg squeezed her hair in her fists, then ran her fingers through it to coax it away from her face. She pulled out her shirt tail and wrung water from it. There was nothing she could do about her jeans, which were dripping into her socks and muddy sneakers. The next bolt of lightning lit the shed so that Meg could see Piet grinning at her.

"Welcome to my castle," he said. "Rest yourself here on my antique couch." He pushed her down into a sitting position while he continued to stand above her, leaning his head on a hand that was against one of the low rafters.

She felt all around her. The "couch" was a stack of burlap and plastic bags. She moved to the edge of the stack. "It's elegant," she said. "Won't you join me and tell me what this place is."

He hesitated and then he sat on the other end, leaving as much room as possible between them, two inches at least. "I don't know what it was built to be. Most of this land was farmed in the early days, before better land opened up west of here. This building may have been a chicken coop or a toolshed. I discovered it when I was about ten years old and patched it up myself. Mr. Pearce said it could be my hideaway as long as I never built a fire up here. I camped here—with friends and alone. I haven't been here for a very long time. Didn't realize the roof leaked so badly."

"It's leaking all around us but not on us. I think this is pretty cozy."

"I think you're a good sport."

Lightning lit the entire cabin. A cracking sound, amplified a hundredfold, split the air. Meg yelped involuntarily.

"Close, much too close!" Piet jumped to his feet and ran out the door.

"What was it?" She rose to follow him.

"Lightning hit a tree. We've just got to hope that the rain will put out any fire. You stay here."

She didn't want to stay; she was frightened and she wanted to be close to Piet. She took a step toward the door and then returned to the "couch."

He was back in minutes. "I can't see anything."

"Meaning fire?" Meg's voice trembled.

Piet sat down beside her.

She shivered and he put his arm around her and drew her close. "Don't worry, Meg." He rubbed his cheek against her hair. "Lightning strikes whatever reaches highest, in this case any of a number of trees."

"And if one fell?"

"None of the tallest trees is dangerously close to us. I checked when I was out, Meg. We're safe." He hugged her closer.

And then he began to stroke her cold wet arm . . . and her neck . . . and her cheek. "Don't be afraid," he murmured, again and again. He put his other hand on her hip.

A charge, more intense than the lightning outside, went through her. She turned slowly—as if drawn by a magnet—and raised her lips. He kissed her gently. Once. Twice. Three times. The fourth kiss was not gentle and the fifth drained the breath from her lungs. His hands touched her body in places she had not known to be sensitive.

I will yield because I can't do anything else, Meg said to herself. *Yield? She wasn't yielding—a Victorian concept—she was rushing forward eagerly. Her hands and lips were just as active as his. She was responsible for . . .* Simultaneously their hands dropped to their sides. They drew away from one another and turned so that they sat with her back leaning into his back, their shoulders heaving.

He was the first to speak: "I'm sorry."

"Are you? I can't honestly say that I am."

"You're not?" He chuckled. "Then I'm not. I could only be sorry if I had upset you." His voice dropped to a whisper. "I hadn't planned . . . In fact I had planned not to let myself . . . I should stay away from you. I must stay away from you."

"Because of Rick?" she asked.

"He's one reason . . ."

"There are others?"

He didn't answer. They sat in silence as the thunder rumbled off into the distance. Meg cherished the warmth from his back creeping through her damp shirt. She cherished him. He had made her feel such passion as she had never felt before.

"The storm's over but it's still dripping," he said at last.

"You think if we go out we might get wet?" She laughed as they turned toward each other.

"I didn't know there was anyone in the world like you, Meg." He stood and put his hand down to pull her to her feet.

They kissed one another quickly, allowing only their lips to touch. When they had sloshed down to the truck, it refused to start and Meg was glad. She should have been eager to get out of her clammy wet clothes. Instead, she was reluctant to leave this enchanted forest. "Singin' in the Rain," they sang as they tramped hand in hand toward the bridge.

"Thank God," he breathed when they reached the bridge. "I was afraid it might have been washed out."

They walked on into the gardens. Ahead, the house was dark. The house was dark! They began to run toward it, he pulling her along so that her feet barely And touched the ground. *He's the only man I've ever met who's made me feel small,* Meg thought.

"Miss Pearce," Piet began to call, long before she could have heard him. "Miss Pearce?" He was frantic.

"Piet. Meg." She stood in the doorway frowning at them. "I told you there'd be a storm. I told you not to go up there. You wouldn't listen to me. You are both willful and obstinate and. . . . And I'm so glad to see you." She reached out her arms to Piet and hugged him and then reached around him to clasp Meg's hand.

"So why is it dark in here?" he asked.

"Power's off. What do you think?"

Meg took off her muddy shoes and socks and was entering the door when the village fire siren began to wail.

"I take it the truck is mired in the mud, so take the car," Miss Pearce said. "Piet's a volunteer fireman," she explained to Meg as they went inside. "Pump isn't working but I filled my bathtub before the power went out. It's probably cold by now but you can at least wash the mud off." She stopped and peered up at Meg. "You look mighty chipper for someone who's spent the last several hours out in a storm."

"We weren't out. We were in a funny little building that Piet said had been his hideaway when he was a child. The roof leaked some but it was . . . cozy. We got pretty wet getting there and then when we got to the truck it wouldn't start so we had to walk back. But we were already so wet it didn't matter."

Miss Pearce led her to a large, modern bathroom and handed her a stack of thick, fluffy towels.

An hour later, Meg heard the car on the gravel, but Piet did not come to the house. Instead, he phoned Miss Pearce to tell her that a barn fire had been put out, with the help of the rain, and that he expected to spend the rest of the day at home.

Doesn't he want to see me? Meg asked herself. She knew the answer: *He does not.* She lay back in a huge chair in the garden room, unaware of Miss Pearce who was sitting nearby, watching the return of blue skies.

Meg sat and dreamed until Miss Pearce put a glass of white wine into her hand. Then she tried to make conversation, telling her hostess of the grapevines strangling the evergreens, but her mind kept wandering off to Piet's hideaway. The electricity came back on while they were eating the cold supper the housekeeper had prepared.

Meg went to bed early. *Time to quit dreaming and begin thinking!* She began by thinking about Rick. What had their first quarrel been about? Waiting five years to have a child? Buying instead of renting an apartment? Was either of those an insurmountable problem? Neither was.

What really confused her was the fact that Rick had wanted to set a marriage date *after* he had lied to her about spending a week in Chicago. Did he think that she would not have understood his return to the Berkshires to continue to court the Webster account? She laughed ruefully; she wouldn't have understood. She'd have been jealous and mad at Jocelyn, who was probably the innocent victim in this boring old story.

Then there was Piet. Just thinking about his lips on hers filled her with desire. Rick's kisses had always been gentle, tender, never demanding. The pleasure she had enjoyed in his arms seemed tepid, now that she had been fully aroused by Piet.

And Piet? Passionate Piet? She loved . . . No, she lusted for Piet. She liked him, too. But they had nothing basic in common. He was so relaxed, so unambitious, so nice. He was a much nicer, kinder person than she.

She didn't know Piet well enough to love him. She didn't love Rick, either. She no longer trusted him and she had never felt crazed by his kisses. Any further relationship with either brother was out of the question. What could be cruder than to switch her affections from one man to his brother? Surely there was a taboo against such behavior.

The situation was like a pot of cooked spaghetti. She could not separate the pieces or make them lie straight. She dropped her feet to the floor and stepped to the window.

Through the trees, she saw light she knew came from the A-frame. Was Piet lying awake in his bed just beyond the secret garden? She could go to him . . . What she imagined was so enticing that she reached for her robe and started for the door.

With her hand on the knob, she shook her head and forced herself to turn back to the bed. If Piet were lying awake, he was probably thinking about Rick, a brother he did not wish to offend. Piet was an honorable man. Once upon a time, she would have said the same of Rick.

Meg slept fitfully for a few hours and was awake before dawn. As soon as it was light, she went to seek out Miss Pearce and found her drinking coffee in her kitchen. Meg poured herself a mug and sat down opposite the old lady.

"I must go back to the city," she said. "I have enjoyed this vacation more than I can tell you, but . . ." She shook her head, confounded by tears rising behind her gritty eyes. "I can't explain."

"Today?" Miss Pearce asked.

"If possible. There must be a bus from Stockbridge or Great Barrington."

"There is. There is also a train from Hudson. That's the more pleasant trip and hours shorter. I'll check the schedule and ask Piet to drive you."

"I'll take a taxi."

Miss Pearce reached across the table and touched Meg's hand. "Let Piet drive you, my dear."

Meg nodded and they sat in silence until Miss Pearce reached for the phone and Meg went to her room to pack.

She said good-bye to Miss Pearce with regret; she cared for the old lady whom she would probably never see again. Several times that morning while they had toured the gardens checking for storm damage, she had thought of confiding in her, but they were both private people.

Piet loaded her bags in the Mercedes and drove silently into Stonefield, where he pointed to a little mustard-colored clapboard house set close to the road next to the post office. A For Sale sign was attached to the front door. "It's owned by a lawyer who used it for his office," Piet said. "He's gone to Florida."

His voice was gravelly. Meg looked at him for the first time. His eyes were puffy and his skin looked splotchy. "You look terrible," she murmured.

"Well, guess what? I feel terrible. You may think I'm hung over but I'm not. After the fire I bought a pack of cigarettes and I came home and made myself a pot of coffee and I drank coffee and smoked all night long. So I guess I am hung over—on nicotine and caffeine, not liquor."

"I never saw you smoke," she said.

"I don't. I hadn't had a cigarette for five years—until yesterday—and I won't have another."

"If I'd known you had a pack, I might have been over. I guess if you've ever smoked, you want a cigarette when you feel stressed."

"You felt stressed yesterday?" he asked.

"Yes, Piet. And very happy for a while."

"For a while, but not forever. That's a problem, isn't it? I love you, but you're my brother's girl. You are also a lawyer. And I am a fool; I keep dreaming of a life I can't have."

"Why did you show me the law office, Piet?"

"It's part of the dream. I imagined a scene where you'd take one look at it, quit your job in New York, and move here." He laughed without humor.

Meg bit her lip. He'd just said he loved her. If passion and love were synonymous, she loved him. Two weeks ago, she had thought she loved Rick. She said nothing.

Piet drove several miles before he spoke again. "I liked working in the arboretum with you and going to Olana and Tanglewood. Sex would be great between us."

"You're right," Meg whispered.

He looked at her and then away. "But dammit all, I don't want a casual fling with my brother's old girlfriend, and that's all it would be for you." His voice was accusing.

"How can you know that?"

"You're not my kind. More to the point, I'm not your kind." His voice was rising. "You've had a nice vacation, playing in the dirt. Now you can clean the dirt out from under your fingernails and go sit behind your big desk in your big office on Madison Avenue."

"Are you saying I'm a fake, like the old masters

at Olana or like plastic flowers? You are wrong. I honestly loved being in Stonefield. I loved the gardens and the arboretum. I loved being with Miss Pearce—and you."

Piet shrugged his shoulders. "Even so, you and Fred will probably patch things up. You're so well suited. If you do, I'll grin like the stupid idiot that I am—"

"Oh, cut the poor-little-me bit. You are a self-educated artist, Piet, and a nice person."

"Sure I'm nice. So nice that I'll be the best man at your wedding and the godfather of your children. Good old Uncle Piet."

Neither of them spoke as they drove through the town of Hudson to the train station. As they turned into the parking lot, the announcement of the train's imminent arrival was blaring over the loudspeaker. Meg ran to buy her ticket while Piet took her bags from the trunk.

When they met at the tracks, they turned to face each other. The sadness in his eyes was a reflection of the sadness in her heart. She leaned forward and kissed him gently. "I will never forget yesterday," she whispered.

She boarded the train and turned to wave, but he was already heading back to the car.

Chapter Thirteen

EVERY bone and nerve in Meg's body wanted to pull the shades in her room, turn up the air conditioner, crawl under the covers, and stay there for three days. Instead she dropped her bags and went out immediately to buy herself good things to eat, and a small bunch of daisies.

She tended her plants. Blythe had watered them while Meg had been in Stonefield, but some were drowning and others were dried out. Every plant had at least a few yellow leaves.

She cleaned her room and the bathroom and did her laundry and changed her sheets. She was busy all evening. She stroked Wally while she watched the eleven o'clock news. He was smooth as silk and even more precious to her now that she knew that Piet had carved him.

Saturday, she resolved to *enjoy* the city, starting at the Metropolitan Museum, which was almost empty on a hot August weekend. She began on the ground level with the fashion exhibit and then went to the main entry and stood for a long time admiring the flower arrangements in enormous urns. Up the broad marble staircase to the Impressionists and down to have lunch at the cafeteria—with a glass of wine. Rested, she studied the catalog of exhibits and went to see the antique musical instruments. The Metropolitan Museum is one of the world's great treasure houses. Again and again she told herself how lucky she was to live within walking distance of it.

The next morning she went to an early church service—where she found no solace—and then to the Central Park Zoo. She strolled from the penguin house, past the white owl and on to the monkey island. The tiny deer, sharing space with red pandas—no relation to Chinese pandas—reminded her of Piet's miniature evergreens. And then she went to the centerpiece of the zoo and watched the sea lions swim and show off for an audience ranging in age from six months to eighty-six. One, bigger than all the rest, flopped up on a rock, looked around and clapped his flippers as if to say, "Aren't I the clever one?" She wished Piet were with her.

Piet, not Rick! Never Rick. After that hour in the storm, she could never be content in Rick's arms. Her afternoon with Piet, exploring an art form neither of them knew anything about, had spoiled her for Rick's reactions, which often seemed to come prepackaged. If Picasso was the person to admire, Rick admired him. If duck confit was this year's rage, Rick ordered it.

Since she did not love Rick, she must terminate whatever remained of their relationship as quickly and as cleanly as possible. She walked a few steps and then she dropped down on a bench and buried her face in her hands.

Separating from Rick would not bring her closer to Piet. Piet had made that clear. He valued his relationship with his brother. Furthermore, although Piet's life had seemed like an idyll, Piet himself was an enigma. He had seemed gentle and unflappable; he did, in fact, have a temper. He seemed self-assured, until he compared himself with his brother. He had said he loved her, and then he had accused her of faking her enthusiasm for the gardens and gardening.

She had not been pretending. Still, she could never devote her life to a garden; she certainly could not move to Stonefield. She had worked too hard to become a "hotshot lawyer." She had no future with either Piet or Rick.

She stood and walked out of the park on leaden feet. Tomorrow she would go back to work. She wondered where they'd put her. Wherever, she'd put all her energy into her work. Beavers may love one another till death, but not humans. Human love never lasts.

When she had paid off her loans and assured herself of a partnership, she might look for a little cottage, not too far from the city, where she could plant a garden. There might never be an Alice for her. So she'd get a dog, she thought ruefully.

When she reached Lexington Avenue, she bought a paper and took it into a small restaurant. She read while she ate a substantial brunch and drank several cups of coffee.

Her phone was ringing as she entered the apartment. Rick was calling from just outside the city.

"I went to Aunt Hat's to pick you up. Where the hell were you? You owe me an explanation, Meg. Meet me at Dino's in an hour."

"I was to phone if I wanted you to pick me up. If you wish to discuss this further, you can come here. I'll be at home for the rest of the day." She hung up.

He was angry when he arrived but finally agreed that he had indeed asked her to call if she wanted a ride home. "Jocelyn tells me you were at Tanglewood with Piet. She is under the impression that you are his girlfriend."

"Did you tell her that I have been engaged to you?"

"Why should I? We're obviously not engaged now." Then he grinned with his mouth only. "I can't believe you'd go out with Piet, but if you wanted a ride to the rehearsal . . ."

"Actually, we went to lunch and swimming after the concert." She picked up Wally and stroked his smooth stomach. "Why didn't you tell me he carved this?"

"The real present was the silver pin on the silk scarf. The walrus was just a little something extra, like a stocking stuffer."

"Do you know that Piet's carvings are sold in the local art gallery?"

"I didn't know." He stood thinking for a moment. "People *buy* Piet's little animals? I wonder what they pay. He could probably do better in the city. I'll talk to him about that. Piet has no business sense."

"I've worn the scarf so I doubt if you'll want it back, but here's the pin." She lifted it from her jewelry box and handed it to him. "You'll have to go to court to get Wally back." She laughed and then sobered. "Did you go to Chicago at all, or did you spend the whole week in the Berkshires?"

"The Berkshires. Look, Meg, I know how you feel about the time I've been spending with the Montgomerys. I didn't want a hassle."

"And Jocelyn thinks that you have been courting her as well as her father. So why were you so insistent on setting a wedding date with me? Why didn't you just let things slide along for a while?"

He stood staring at the floor. Then he looked up and straight into her eyes. "I wanted you, Meg, not Jocelyn. I thought if we had definite plans it would be easier to tell her. She tends to be rather possessive."

"You're blaming her?" Meg went to the door and held it open.

Suddenly he smiled broadly. "It's still a secret—won't be released to the press until Thursday. We're signing on the Webster account. I'll be in charge." He kissed her on the cheek. "Ta-ta."

"Good-bye, Rick. I don't regret the months we spent together. We had some good times."

"And we were a handsome couple, and equally ambitious. I loved that about you. Jocelyn is not ambitious; she doesn't have to be." He turned back and put his hands on her shoulders. "Shall we give it another try? I'll be tied up for the next couple of weeks, but I'll give you a call after Labor Day. How about it?"

"Don't, Rick. It's over."

"But we'll keep in touch?"

"No, Rick, we won't." Meg closed the door behind him.

The next morning, Meg dressed with care for her return to her professional mode. Blythe had described the yellow short-sleeved suit as "both businesslike and feminine, the perfect combination, and absolutely smashing on you." Meg looked at herself in the full-length mirror and thought of Miss Pearce in her coolie suits.

"You're looking spiffy, Meg," Joel said when she entered his office on Monday morning. "Your vacation must have been terrific. Where'd you and Rick go?"

"Rick and I are a thing of the past." Meg was surprised at how easy that was to say. "I went to the Berkshires and spent two weeks helping an old woman with her gardens. I also went to Tanglewood and Olana. It was a good vacation. How are things here?"

"Good. Dixon's accumulated almost six percent of Smengine's stock and the paperwork's all in at the SEC. We busted our buns around here last week, but it's done." He spoke with enthusiasm and pride. Joel really cared that they had done the necessary filings for the client.

"And when is your vacation?"

"Friday until after Labor Day. We're going to Maine to do absolutely nothing."

Meg reported to Mr. Spencer, who prolonged the questions about her vacation to the point where she was beginning to suspect that what he had to say to her was not something she wanted to hear. Indeed it was not.

The president of one of their major client companies had a daughter who had been arrested early that morning for drug possession. "It's our job—your job, in fact—to get her released and then to get the charges dropped. As you can imagine, Jackson does not want any word of this to leak to the media."

"First offense?"

Mr. Spencer shook his head. "No," he mouthed. "We've been through this before, several times. By the end of today you'll wish you were back with us in good old gray mergers and acquisitions. The girl's name is Prudence, which is sadly inappropriate. She must be seventeen now. Mouth like a garbage can. Morals of an alley cat. We thought, actually Savage thought, you might be able to handle her better than others have handled her in the past. You are diplomatic, he says. Frankly, I don't think diplomacy will do you much good. Just get her out and into a treatment center."

"How many treatment centers has she been in so far?" Meg asked suspiciously.

"Too many."

"And why are we handling the case? Why don't we just refer the father to a firm that specializes in these kinds of cases?"

"Because Jackson knows us to be discreet and his company is our largest single source of revenue. I'm sorry, Meg. Somebody has to do the ugly jobs. Once. You'll never be asked again, if that consoles you."

Prudence was relatively pleasant for a few moments after entering the room where she was to talk to her lawyer. All she needed, she told Meg, was a little crack. Meg judged her weight at about ninety pounds, her skin was sallow and marked with acne. Her hair, greasy brown with a single streak of green, appeared to have been cut with pinking shears.

When Meg had convinced her that she had not come bearing crack, or any other drug, the girl's vocabulary degenerated to a level that Meg had not imagined possible. To compare her mouth to a garbage can was to insult the can. She shrieked invectives against Meg, the police, the mayor, the President and God. But she knew the system, and when they were standing before the judge she cried pitifully while Meg asked to be allowed to take her to a private facility in New Jersey until her next court appearance.

The family doctor was waiting in the limo parked outside of the court. He gave the girl a shot and stepped out on the sidewalk. Prudence slept while the family chauffeur drove her and Meg through the Lincoln Tunnel and out Route 22 to a rural area that Meg judged to be near the Delaware River.

At last, they drove to a gate with a small brass sign identifying the place as Sunny Acres. When the gate was unlocked, they continued down a long drive toward an old mansion. Two burly young men were at the end of the drive. They reached into the limo and pulled Prudence out and into a semi-upright position. A man in a white coat stood on the steps and watched impassively.

Meg jumped out of the car and approached the man, who was obviously a doctor. She extended her hand and introduced herself as Prudence's lawyer. "What is this place? What will you do for her?"

"We'll detoxify her and give her another chance," the doctor said wearily. "When does she have to be back in court?"

Meg named the date and he nodded.

"I hope you do more than just detoxify her," Meg said. "You must try to—"

"We try. We can keep her off drugs for the time she is with us. We can drag her to counseling sessions. We can lecture her endlessly on how she is hurting herself more than she is hurting her father, which I suspect is the point of all this, or was in the beginning. We cannot cure her unless she wants to be cured." He turned away from Meg and followed the two guards and Prudence through the door.

The teenager looked pathetic, a dirty rag bag hanging limply while the toes of her one-hundred-fifty-dollar running shoes scuffed along the marble hallway toward a graceful open stairway.

Neither Meg nor the chauffeur spoke all the way back to the city except when he asked her where she wanted to be dropped and she gave him her address.

Meg washed her hair and stood under the shower for thirty minutes and still she felt dirty. Later in the evening, she called Mr. Jackson at home; she had been instructed never to call him at his office. She told him that Prudence had been delivered and that she had to be back in court on September 18.

"I won't be there, of course, but her

mother . . ." He gave her the mother's current name and phone number. "Just keep her out of jail."

"May I tell the judge that she'll have a home with you?" Meg asked.

"You can tell him that if necessary, but of course . . . You just find a school for her. Someplace out of town. Anyplace that will take her will be expensive but don't worry. Just have them bill me, at home." He paused. Was he waiting for Meg to congratulate him on his generosity? She said nothing. "Thank you, Miss Bower. Was that the name? I'm counting on you to be discreet. Good night." He hung up.

The next morning, Mr. Spencer asked her about her encounter with Prudence.

Meg described her day and her late-night call to the father. "In one breath Mr. Jackson suggested I call her mother and in the next he ordered me to find a school for her, so I guess he doesn't expect much from the mother. By the way, did anyone tell him that I am a lawyer, not a psychologist or a social worker? How would I find a school?"

"You call an agency or a professional and you pay them for their advice. Ask my secretary to find out who we used last time."

"May I use a classmate of mine? She specializes in adolescents."

"Anyone you choose. Prudence will only take a few hours of your time. Find a school or an institution or whatever. If she asks to see you before her court appearance, go. That's it. In the meantime, the tax department is shorthanded."

Until yesterday, Meg would have been dismayed by an assignment to the tax department. One day with Prudence was enough to change her mind. Numbers don't talk back or demand sympathy. They can be left in the computer and forgotten at night.

Meg dialed Prudence's mother. Whoever it was who answered said that she was out of reach. She was not expected back until early October.

Meg's classmate, who was establishing a private practice in the city, was the first person to express any concern for Prudence. "No seventeen-year-old is beyond redemption, Meg."

"I hope you'll still say that after you've met this one. The doctor I talked to at Sunny Acres, which is a classy detox center, suggested that she's trying to get her father's attention. Some maneuver, if you ask me."

"Is she bright?"

"I don't know. Her vocabulary is limited to about twenty of the most vile words in the English language, but she knew enough to keep her mouth shut and cry when she stood before the judge."

"Please ask her father to call Sunny Acres and authorize them to speak to me. Later I'll go talk to Prudence. Then I'll try to set up a meeting with her parents and suggest possible therapies. There are a couple of really fine schools for kids like this."

Having put Prudence in capable—and caring—hands, Meg reported to the tax department, which was, indeed, shorthanded.

Chapter Fourteen

A box that had been delivered during the day was waiting for her when she got home from work late Friday evening. Presents thrilled Meg. She opened the box and carefully removed popped corn to reveal a spray of fragile lilies nestled against a feathery pine bough. Smiling at their beauty, she lifted them from the box. Beneath, protected by bubble wrap, were six luscious tomatoes. She took one to the kitchen immediately, leaned over the sink and ate the whole thing. It was the best tomato she had ever eaten. Under the tomatoes was a folded piece of paper. Inside Piet had drawn a grapevine around a disappointingly brief note: "Meg, I'm sorry. Piet."

Four words. How she wished he'd written more. He might have addressed her as "dear" or signed off with a "love," or "affectionately." Still his note and this gift gave her the excuse she wanted. She lifted the phone and dialed information for Piet's number. He was not at home. She tried again Saturday morning before she went to the office and again in the afternoon and at night. She finally reached him on Sunday afternoon.

"Oh Piet. Thank you. The tomatoes are the best I ever ate. The lilies are beautiful. You know—"

He interrupted her. "Fred's here."

"Is he? Then you may know that he and I have made a clean and final break."

"He told me. Good-bye, now." He hung up, leaving her to stare at the silent phone.

How dare he pretend they were strangers discussing the weather! Even if Rick were standing right at his elbow, he wouldn't have had to hang up on her.

Monday, Meg did not get home until after ten. There was no message on her machine from Piet or anyone else. Nor on Tuesday. Nor any day that week. She concentrated on her work, which was very interesting, she told herself repeatedly.

Sunday morning she phoned him again. "I don't understand, Piet," she said simply.

At least he didn't pretend not to know what she was talking about. "I guess I was a bit abrupt last Sunday. Fred was in the room."

"So why didn't you phone me back? My name's in the book."

A long silence. "There's nothing to say, Meg." More silence. "Until last weekend, I had assumed you were a sort of trainee lawyer. Boy was I wrong! Rick told me how much money you make. *You* should have let me know, instead of pretending to be interested in my life. Good-bye, Attorney Bower."

"Don't hang up on me, Piet. Not until I've had my

say. When I was in Stonefield, I was happier than I can ever remember being in my whole life. Believe that, or not, as you choose. And I don't particularly like my work. How many times do I have to tell you that?"

"Tell your troubles to your bankbook." His voice was the voice of a stranger.

Meg hung up the phone.

The next day, Labor Day, Meg went to a picnic at the home of one of her law-school friends. The train trip to Larchmont only took thirty minutes. She walked through shaded streets to the large Victorian house painted light blue with Chinese red trim. The hostess, who practiced law with her father, was married to a stockbroker. They had a two-year-old son. *Who says you can't have it all?* Meg asked herself.

Later, she asked the question of her schoolmate, who laughed contentedly. "I do have everything, don't I?"

Meg nodded. "You also seem very happy and I am glad for you. Tell me about your work."

"I work about four hours a day and we handle whatever needs to be done, mostly real estate transactions and estates, an occasional damage suit. It's not as exciting or as lucrative as corporate law, but I like it. And if the baby is sick or the sitter doesn't show up, I stay home. I'm a very lucky woman, Meg. And you? Last time I saw you, you were about to become engaged to a Dutch Adonis."

"That's over. I don't know what to tell you about me. I'm still looking for my niche in the firm. I've been floating. Taxes right now. Contrary to what you have heard, life in a corporate law firm is often tedious. And while I'm in my poor-little-me mode, let me tell you that I don't like living in the city, certainly not in the summer."

"Where would you rather live?"

"Right there." Meg pointed to a little shed with hollyhocks growing along one side. "Anyplace surrounded by green."

"Then move out here. Shall I give you the names of a couple of realtors?"

Meg laughed. "Not yet."

That night, and during free moments during the following week, Meg deliberately replaced thoughts of Piet with pictures of a little cottage surrounded by flowers within walking distance of a train station that would be less than an hour from the city.

On Tuesday, her mail included a lavishly illustrated garden catalog. "Last chance to order bulbs for spring blooming." There were more different daffodils and tulips than she had imagined possible and other bulbs that were completely new to her.

She also went to dinner and the theater with a stockbroker she had met at the Larchmont picnic. He was recently divorced and eager to get through the pleasantries and back to his apartment. When she refused to accompany him, she knew she'd never hear from him again. She didn't care.

The next week she received three more garden catalogs. She took one of them with her when she and

Jane were driven to New Jersey to talk to Prudence on the Thursday before her court appearance.

Jane strode into the room where Prudence sat huddled behind a table. "Hello, Prudence. My name is Jane Mitchem. I'm a psychotherapist. Are you clean?"

Prudence looked up at her and nodded vaguely. She seemed diminished, plainer, with only a trace of green left in her limp hair, and thinner. And then a spark of the old Prudence flashed across her face and she let go with a string of shocking words ending with "Damned if I want to be clean."

"Okay," Jane said. "If you don't want to stay off drugs, there's nothing I or your lawyer can do for you. I doubt that you'll find jail much to your liking, but it's the one therapy you haven't tried. Come on, Meg. If we hurry we can be back in the city for lunch." She headed for the door.

Bewildered, Meg followed. They were through the door when Prudence made a noise more like a mew than a word.

"You say something?" Jane asked without turning around.

"Come back, you two. . . ."

Jane stood quietly until the stream of obscenities dwindled to silence and then she handed the girl information about three schools. "I thought that it might be a good idea for *you* to pick your school this time." She began to describe the facilities, opening one of the brochures in front of the girl.

"What does my father think?" Prudence's voice was surly.

"He wants you to choose," Jane said quickly.

Mr. Jackson's response to the same brochures had been dismissive. "Let your shrink friend pick the place," he'd said. "That's what I'm paying her for."

Jane went on describing each of the places and, at last, the girl began to leaf through the printed material. "What do you think?" she asked Meg.

Meg shook her head. "I don't know anything about these kinds of places . . ."

"You probably went to a la-di-da school like Bryn Mawr or Holyoke." Prudence was accusing.

"Smith. So did Dr. Mitchem."

"My sister's at Holyoke," Prudence said. "She's a good girl. She doesn't even say 'hell' and she'd never have the nerve to smoke a cigarette. Oh, heavens no. Not sweet little Joy."

The fact that Prudence had a sister was news to Meg.

"Joy doesn't interest me," Jane said. "You do. If you want my advice, I'd suggest that you try the school in Lenox, Massachusetts. Pretty country up there. The school is housed in one of the old mansions and has beautiful grounds. But it's tough, maybe too tough for you. You get caught with drugs just once and you'll be out. No second chances. You'll also be expected to clean up your vocabulary. On the other hand, they're loving. Everyone from the director down hugs everyone else."

"Sap-py," Prudence said disdainfully.

"Probably. Many of the students, however, missed out on hugs when they were children. Shall I tell them to make up a bed for you?"

"Locks?"

"No." Jane waited until Prudence nodded, then she turned to Meg. "You can tell the judge we've found a fine facility that will give your client every opportunity to clean up her act."

Meg talked to Prudence for a few minutes but the girl knew more about what to expect in court than Meg did. While they were talking, Prudence fingered the garden catalog Meg had laid on the table. Although the girl appeared to show no interest in it, Meg noticed that the pages flipped over, one by one.

"I love flowers and trees," Meg said. "Do you?"

"Not much. 'Cept marijuana. I grew that in my dad's apartment. Boy, did that throw his wife. That was his second wife, not the one he's with now. She was afraid their precious little crapping boy would get it." Prudence closed the catalog and pushed it across the table.

Meg left the catalog behind.

On the eighteenth, the judge gave Prudence a *pro forma* lecture about not wishing to see her again and about how fortunate she was to have parents who could afford a school that cost thousands of dollars per month. And then she turned Prudence over to Meg with directions to see that she was in the Lenox school by the close of the day.

Prudence received another lecture from her father who, to Meg's surprise, was waiting for them in the limousine that would take them to the airport. The girl appeared not to listen and, at last, Jackson patted her awkwardly on the shoulder and got out in front of his office building. The chauffeur drove them on out to the small airport near LaGuardia where the two of them boarded a company jet. By the time they had eaten their box lunches, they were landing in Pittsfield, where another limousine was waiting.

From time to time, Meg had tried, without success, to make conversation with Prudence. Most of the trip passed in silence. In response to Meg's question, the driver said that it would not be out of the way to drive to Lenox via Stonefield.

"This is one of my favorite towns," Meg said as they approached. "See that ugly pond. A family of beavers live in it. The old couple—beavers mate for life—are named Myrna and William after two old movie stars—"

"—Myrna Loy and William Powell. I used to watch a lot of old movies."

"That gallery over there has some interesting—" Meg stopped and stared at the mustard-colored house on the other side of the street. The For Sale sign was gone and the flower boxes under the first-floor windows had been planted with mums and decorative kale. Meg turned away abruptly. Prudence was studying her face.

Meg forced a grin. "Let's ask the driver to stop at the store for ice-cream cones. Okay? What flavor? They have most of the usual."

Jane had warned Meg that Prudence might try to escape, so Meg left the girl locked in the car with the driver while she went for the cones. As she crossed the sidewalk, she looked up and down; it was deserted. When she entered the store she peered down each of the three aisles. As she entered the car with the cones, she again looked for

Piet. She had not expected to see him, she told herself.

"Here we are," Meg said sometime later as they turned through open gates into a long driveway. "The flower beds are attractive. Looks like kids are working in that one. Do you suppose they are students—"

"Cut the crap, Miz Lawyer Lady. Those kids are patients. I'll be a patient. Not a student. A patient. At least it's a place easy to run away from. Tell my old man that. He doesn't like places without fences or walls."

"I hope you won't want to run away, Prudence." Meg knew that she sounded odiously prim and proper. She took the girl's hand, but Prudence pulled it away and stared straight ahead.

As at Sunny Acres, a welcoming committee waited on the front steps, a bearded middle-aged man who looked like a teddy bear, three girls about Prudence's age, and two boys. As soon as the car stopped, Meg leaped out and motioned for Prudence to follow. She was determined that no one would drag the girl from the car this time. No one tried. The six greeters stayed on the steps until Meg and Prudence were walking toward them and then they ran forward, smiling broadly.

The middle-aged man introduced himself as the director. "We are so very glad to have you join us, Prudence," he said as he drew her toward him and kissed her cheek.

Prudence looked terrified, as if she had seen a monster rising from the grass beyond the director's shoulder. She didn't move a muscle. She didn't even blink her eyes. When the director released her, an owlish-looking girl stepped forward, her eyes lowered, as she touched Prudence's arms for a moment and whispered one word: "Welcome."

"Hey, Prudence," the next girl cried, grinning broadly and hugging the newcomer warmly. She kissed her on both cheeks. "You rather be called Pru? Just let me know. We aim to please. This is your roommate. Come here, Cecelia, and meet Prudence."

The girl named Cecelia stepped forward and smiled shyly. "Welcome," she said. "I'm new, too." She shook Prudence's hand.

Both of the boys hugged her and then the greeters picked up her bags and headed into the house. Prudence still stood looking stunned. Then she turned to Meg, rummaged in her large bag, and pulled out the catalog.

"You may keep it," Meg said hastily.

Prudence thrust it at Meg.

"You like growing things?" the director asked.

Prudence countered with a question of her own. "Why all the damned hugging? It's stupid."

"Lots of people would agree with you. In our culture we usually hug and kiss children until they are about eight years old. Then we stop except for special occasions. But we have students here who have never been hugged and kissed. When we do it, we're just demonstrating that, no matter what happened in the past, we care about one another now. Try it for a while. You may like it. Say goodbye to your friend and get yourself settled before dinner." The director turned toward the front door.

"She's not my friend; she's my lawyer. My dad's

paying her to keep me out of jail." Prudence marched into the house behind the director.

"So long, Prudence," Meg called after her.

Meg felt bereft. She had thought she would be glad to be rid of Prudence. She had thought she would enjoy seeing Stonefield again. She bit her lip and blinked her eyes but she did not cry. Meg Bower was not a crier.

That evening, while giving Mr. Jackson her report on the phone, she had a sudden idea. "Prudence appears to enjoy plants," Meg said. "Maybe you'll want to send her a houseplant for her room."

"Good idea!" The father sounded so enthusiastic that Meg was about to congratulate herself—prematurely. "Order something nice and put it on my bill. Good-bye. Let's just hope she's out of our hair for a few months, anyway."

"Would you like an evaluation from Dr. Mitchem? She feels quite optimistic about your daughter's future."

"I don't have time to read a lot of psychological jargon. I'll believe Prudence is on the right track when she begins to behave herself." He hung up, leaving Meg to curse the phone.

The next day, Meg went to a florist on Madison Avenue, intending to have a plant wired to Prudence. She left without buying one. That night she phoned Piet. He sounded surprised to hear her voice. Was he also pleased? She couldn't tell. "I heard you were in town, Meg," he said.

"Are there no secrets in Stonefield? I only stopped long enough to buy an ice-cream cone."

"Three ice-cream cones, two chocolate, one

strawberry, which you took to a stretch limousine."

Meg laughed and then told Piet about Prudence. "She's one of the most unpleasant young women I have ever met," she concluded, "but she couldn't keep her hands off the bulb catalog I had with me when I visited her in New Jersey. Her father's agreed to send her a houseplant. He doesn't care what it costs, so long as he's not inconvenienced."

"Nice man, huh?"

"Actually, he's a very successful businessman and he has a straitlaced older daughter who is in college . . . Believe me, it's not easy to like Prudence, though the psychologists think she's acting out to get his attention. She's not succeeding."

"Is her room sunny?" Piet asked.

"Oh, Piet, I just don't have any idea. I could call the school."

"I'll call the school. Girl's name is Prudence Jackson? Maybe a terrarium with several different foliage plants and a gloxinia for color. . . ."

"That sounds perfect. She couldn't help but like it. Thank you. Send me the bill and I'll pass it on to the father."

For a moment neither of them spoke.

"Are you okay?" Piet finally asked.

"I'm okay, Piet. I noticed that the law office in Stonefield has been sold."

"Yes. Have you seen Fred lately?"

"No. He hasn't called. I don't wish him to."

"He will. It was good to hear from you, Meg. I'll phone when I've made the delivery." He hung up the phone.

Don't hang up, Piet. Talk to me. Invite me to come back to Stonefield. Meg's eyes were moist.

On Friday, an assistant district attorney she had met a few times previously phoned to invite her to dinner on Saturday. She said she had other plans. When she had hung up, she acknowledged her own stupidity. Piet would not call until he had delivered the plant or the terrarium to Prudence, which would probably be sometime during the following week. Besides, why should she wait around for him to call?

Piet called late Saturday afternoon. After a perfunctory greeting, he sighed. "You were right, Meg. She is nasty. I took the terrarium to the office and waited while someone went to find her. I couldn't put the usual card on it because I didn't know what she calls her father."

"Probably 'he' or 'him.' "

"When she got to the office, I told her that her father had asked me to deliver the terrarium to her. She curled her lip and said, 'He did not. That chic lawyer he hired probably ordered it for him.' "

"At least she said I was chic. That's something."

"You are chic, Meg. I sometimes wish. . . . Never mind. I tried to tell Prudence how to care for the plants but she refused to even look at them. I don't know if she heard me or not, so I just left my card and told her to phone me if she had any questions. I was almost to the truck when she came running after me, suddenly full of thanks. She just *loved* it."

Something about the way Piet drew out the word

"love" made Meg suspicious. "She wasn't being sincere?"

"I wasn't sure until she did a pathetic imitation of a streetwalker. I can't remember exactly what she said next but she let me know that she wasn't particular about her drugs, anything would do—pot, crack, whiskey."

"Oh, Piet, I am sorry. What did you say to her?"

"I told her that I deal in plants, not drugs, and drove off. She's sure one poor little rich girl."

"I guess the city is full of such children."

"There are plenty like her in the country, but few who are rich. Too bad all of them can't be sent to a place like the one she's in. I've always thought the grounds were pleasant. Some magnificent very old beeches. It's nice inside too, or at least the part I saw. I've heard that many of their kids turn out okay. Do you do much of this kind of work, Meg?"

"First and last time. The father is one of our best clients and we do what we can for the daughter because he asks us to. I was stuck with her because someone had to do it. I was hoping she'd have a chance this time. Your report makes me doubt it." There was another brief silence, broken, this time, by Meg. "I'm planning to go to the Frick Museum tomorrow. Want to come down and go with me?"

"Yes," he said softly. "I want to come down, but I won't. Good-bye, Meg."

Chapter Fifteen

THE following Friday night, Meg went out with the assistant district attorney. He took her to Windows on the World where the food was pretentious, the prices astronomical, and the views spectacular. As soon as they had ordered, he began a verbal essay on his future political career.

"I'll need a wife who is bright, attractive—"

"An Elizabeth Dole clone?" Meg asked.

"Right."

"And two children, a lovable little boy with a teddy bear and a little girl with ruffled dresses? And an attractive dog like Milly Bush?"

"Exactly!" His eyes shone. "You understand perfectly, Meg, and you are attractive and bright. Harvard. I don't suppose you were deprived as a child? I need someone who will mitigate my 'silver spoon' image."

Meg stared at him, fascinated. This man was not only intense; he was utterly humorless. He didn't suspect that he was being teased. If she dared to tell him about her background—perfect for his purposes—he might kidnap her and hold her in chains until they were married and on their way to Washington. She changed the subject, ate as quickly as possible, and developed a convenient headache.

"When can I see you again?" he asked as he delivered her to her door. "Tomorrow?"

"Never," she said, but perhaps she spoke too softly.

"I want to see you every day. You are so . . . perfect, Meg. So just right for me."

She couldn't resist the temptation to prove her perfection to Mr. Pompous. "I was on welfare during part of my childhood, too."

"Really? Oh Meg, that's fantastic. You were really on welfare? I can't believe it."

As he waxed on about the advantages of welfare, she began to pity him. "Hear me. I have no—I repeat, no—interest in a political career, either on my own or as the devoted wife of a dedicated young senator. I will vote. I might even contribute five dollars to the campaign of a politician who impressed me. Nothing more. Ever."

She had to repeat herself several times before he heard and accepted the finality of what she said.

Rick called during the following week, just to see how she was. He'd been terribly busy with the Webster account, he said. He'd also spent a long weekend golfing at the Greenbriar. "And you? How are things at the three S's?"

"As usual. Not quite such long hours."

"You're back in mergers?"

"No. Taxes, at present."

"But you see your buddies in mergers. How's your mystery client?"

"I don't know. Since I haven't heard anything to the contrary, I suppose there have been no surprises."

"Let's keep in touch, Meg. Maybe have dinner? I'll call."

Meg discovered that she was smiling as she hung up. There was something so light about Rick. He lifted her spirits, which was more than she could say about either the stockbroker or the assistant district attorney.

In October, those who love New York become rapturous; those who dislike it usually find it tolerable and often attractive. Summer odors and dirt disappear and the air becomes crisp and fresh. Clothing in shop windows and on pedestrians may be elegant or humorous or simply colorful. People smile. The world's greatest artists arrive in theaters, concert halls, and museums.

Meg was not immune to the charms of New York in October. She went to the ballet in Lincoln Center with a friend from the office. One Saturday afternoon, Amy left the baby with her husband and she and Meg went to a new Broadway play. Nights when she could not sleep, which was almost every night, she read mysteries.

After a visit to the Whitney, Meg phoned Piet to tell him about an exhibit he would have hated. He responded so little that she began to feel like a babbling brook and hung up within minutes of placing the call.

* * *

On a Thursday night in mid-October, Meg had dinner with Rick. She sat across the table from him and thought that he was one of the most handsome men she had ever seen. He told her a joke and she thought that he was one of the most amusing men she had ever met. He asked intelligent questions about her work and she thought what a good conversationalist he was. After dinner he invited her back to his room. She refused. She didn't care if she never saw him again; she could attend his wedding to someone else, even Jocelyn, without a pang of jealousy.

They were both silent as they walked the few blocks to her apartment house. They had arrived at her outside door when he spoke. "I saw old Piet last weekend. He was having coffee with a local divorcée. Nice-looking woman in a coarse sort of way. Ta-ta," He kissed her cheek and ran off, leaving Meg standing motionless in front of the door with her key in the lock.

Friday the skies were leaden; Meg felt leaden. Aware that she was not concentrating well, she worked slowly and very carefully, checking and rechecking. About four o'clock, one of the partners came to her office.

"Surely you've completed those forms, Meg. Where are they?"

Meg shook her head. "I'm sorry," she whispered.

"They were routine."

"They'll be waiting on your desk Monday morning."

He looked at her curiously—Meg had the reputation for thorough work delivered on time. He wished her a happy weekend and left.

The leaden skies were dripping mournfully when Meg set out for work on Saturday morning. Soon after noon, she delivered the completed papers to the partner's office and stood looking through sheets of rain to the near-black skies. She felt too tired to move. Her muscles ached.

Deciding that she was probably coming down with the flu or a cold, she went back to her own office and belted her raincoat around her. On her way to the subway she stopped at a bookstore and bought a Josephine Tey mystery. At the other end of the subway she stopped at a grocery store and bought sick food, juice and soup.

At home she put on a pair of faded flannel pajamas and went to bed with her book. The phone rang but she did not answer it—that's what answering machines were for. Blythe came home but Meg did not call to her. She did not see her roommate until evening, when she went to the kitchen to heat a can of soup.

"You sick?" Blythe asked, instantly concerned. Meg nodded her response. "Sore throat?" Meg shook her head. "Fever?" When Meg again shook her head, Blythe looked at her critically. "You need a haircut. You know that, don't you?"

Meg took her soup from the microwave and padded off to her room with it.

Later, Blythe knocked on her door and entered wearing a black jumpsuit and a dozen or more ropes of pearls. "It's a grim, nasty night, Meg, but I'm going to a party. Why don't you come along with me? Change of scenery and all that. Might do you good."

Meg thanked her and asked her to pick up the *Times* on her way home. She went back to her mystery.

By Sunday evening, when she had finished the mystery and the *Times*, Meg admitted that she was not sick after all. At least not physically. *I'm sick in my head and I've been sick off and on for several weeks.* She hadn't finished her work on time because she had felt too lethargic to push herself. She'd felt like this when she came home from delivering Prudence, but that was a day to drop anyone in the dumps. She was feeling better when she went off to have dinner at Windows on the World. She remembered the evening more vividly than was comfortable. She had told that odious man that she had been on welfare. She never told anyone about her childhood. So why had she told him? Because he was such a . . . The word that came to her mind was one Prudence would have used.

She'd known all week that her hair needed cutting but she'd been too lethargic to make an appointment. She'd enjoyed Thursday's dinner with Rick, and afterward it had felt great to be free of him. She should be happy. She got out of bed and played back the messages waiting on her answering machine. One was from Jane wanting to know if she'd heard anything about Prudence.

"Not a thing," Meg said when she called her back. "So at least she must not have run away. I guess that's something." She went on to tell how the girl had behaved when she received the terrarium.

"And you, Meg? How are you? What have you been doing?"

"I spent the weekend in bed. I thought I was coming down with something but I guess I'm okay."

"You don't sound okay. How have you been sleeping during the last couple of weeks?"

"Not so well."

"You working efficiently?"

"Slowly, but accurately."

"More slowly than usual?"

"Yes, but that's enough questions, Miz Shrink."

"You have a reason to be depressed?"

Suddenly Meg was angry at Jane, who wouldn't stop asking questions Meg didn't want to answer. "I was on welfare when I was a child," she shouted into the phone. "You didn't know that, did you? The hotshot lawyer, graduate of Smith and Harvard, was a welfare recipient." Just as suddenly as her anger had flared, it died. "Oh Jane, I am sorry. Really and truly sorry."

"It's all right, Meg. I'm glad you confided in me. If you'd like to come in and talk with me, or with a therapist I could recommend—"

"Thanks, but no thanks. I don't have time."

"Well, *take* time to look at whatever it is that is bothering you and if you continue to sleep poorly and feel lethargic, let me know. There are medications that could make you feel better in just a few weeks."

"Thanks again." Meg hung up. *How could I have talked that way to Jane? Why was I so angry?*

She listened to the rest of her messages. One was from the assistant district attorney; she refused to answer that one. The others could be ignored. She was about to crawl back into bed when she happened to glance at her calendar and gasped. "It's Betsy's tenth birthday today and I forgot," she said aloud.

She sank down on her desk chair and buried her head in her hands for a few minutes. *I am sick in the head.* She grabbed the phone and dialed a number in Vermont. *What am I going to tell her? That I forgot my own niece's birthday, because Piet had coffee with a divorcée?* At the other end of the line she heard the phone ring once, twice. Barry answered on the fifth ring. His voice sounded sleepy. Meg looked at the clock and groaned. It was after eleven; she'd blundered again.

"Oh Barry, I am so sorry. I forgot Betsy's birthday until just now and then I forgot to look at the clock. I've been . . . Please forgive me, Barry, and tell Betsy I'll get a package off to her right away. Any idea what she'd like?"

"She always likes your presents, Peggy. All three of the kids do. They ask about you often."

"What do you tell them?"

"That you're busy but that you'll come see them soon."

"That must be hard for them to swallow." Meg straightened her shoulders. "Tell Betsy I'll *bring* her present to her on Friday if I can get away; if not, on Saturday. If that's okay with you and Barb."

"It's okay with us but I think we'll wait to tell the children . . ."

"Because you're afraid I might not show up."

"You could have to work. Or something could come up."

"I'll be there, Barry. That's a promise."

"I could meet you in Greenfield or Springfield or wherever."

"I'll rent a car. If I can't make it until Saturday, I'll give you a call; otherwise you can count on seeing me Friday afternoon." She paused. "And Barry? I really do want to see all of you."

"I know, Peggy. We want to see you."

Meg, who never cried, blinked and sniffed—and reached for an atlas. She'd never let her driver's license expire but she hadn't driven a car since she'd arrived in New York. What made her think she could possibly make her way through Manhattan and Bronx traffic? It was madness. Furthermore, she dreaded returning to Brinton almost as much as she looked forward to seeing her family.

Chapter Sixteen

To prepare herself for the trip to Brinton, Meg took three hours of driving lessons and reserved a car in Peekskill, well beyond frenzied city traffic. Early Friday morning, she boarded a train at Grand Central that would take her under Manhattan, through the Bronx, and up the Hudson River valley.

When she had arranged her bags in the rack above her, she tilted the seat back and tried to control a flood of regret, anxiety, and anticipation. She had not been in Brinton for more than ten years. She'd had an excuse as long as she was in school; she had to work vacations. She'd spent all summer every summer waiting tables at a resort on Cape Cod, where her hours were long but the tips were good. During the school year she had worked at restaurants in Northampton and then in Boston. On major holidays, especially Christmas, customers were very generous.

While she was at Smith, Barry and Barb and the two older children, John and Betsy, had driven down to Northampton at least once a year and to attend her graduation. When she was in law school, they and the infant Katy had met her in Worcester or Lowell. The last time she had seen them, Katy had been a toddler; she was almost six now.

Meg had no one to blame but herself and her pride. Ten years ago, when she might still have been excused for her foolishness, she had vowed never to return to Brinton unless she could return in style. She'd be driving a red Porsche and wearing a dazzling fur, with diamonds in her earlobes and on her fingers. The original dream had been amended over the years. In her most recent dreams, when she should have outgrown such childish nonsense, she was still driving the red Porsche down Main Street, but she was wearing an elegant suit and cultured pearls.

The dream of the triumphant return had been born on the day she graduated from the consolidated high school. She was wearing a white dress she had bought for seven dollars at the thrift shop in Brattleboro. Her valedictory speech had gone well, and afterward people had gathered around her, shaking her hand and congratulating her.

"How nice you look in that dress," Sharon Davis had exclaimed loudly. "I've always liked it but it didn't look nearly as pretty on my sister as it does on you."

Meg had longed to smash the smirk right into Sharon's fleshy face—which is exactly what she had done when they had been in the third grade. Everyone had been discussing whose mother would make what for the Valentine's Day party—

everyone except eight-year-old Meg, who had slid down in her seat, hoping to be invisible.

When it was Sharon's turn to speak, she had said that her mother would make cupcakes with pink frosting. Then she had turned and smiled sweetly at Meg. "Poor Peggy can't bring anything because her mother went away."

Meg had jumped to her feet and punched Sharon in the nose. As she was running out of the room she had heard Sharon's wails and a simpering voice saying "Poor Peggy. My mother says we should feel very sorry for her."

Meg had run all the way home and her father had held her in his arms for a long time. When she had looked up into his face she had seen tears in his eyes. She had not known that fathers could cry.

Much as she had hated Sharon Davis, she had hated the welfare lady even more.

"What a cozy trailer," the welfare lady had cooed the first time she visited them. "Are you the little homemaker, Peggy?"

She was, but she didn't say so.

"And do you do the cooking, too?"

She didn't, but she often had to do the shopping, which was the most humiliating experience of her young years; she paid with food stamps. Meg laughed without amusement as she remembered the disguise she affected on shopping days, huge sunglasses so dark she could scarcely see the shelves inside the grocery store, a red scarf to cover her hair. Had there been a person in town who had not recognized her and pitied her for trying to pretend that she was someone else?

All those things happened a long time ago, Meg reminded herself as she gathered her bags to leave the train in Peekskill.

The little car she had reserved was not a Porsche, but it was red. She lurched out of the parking lot and stalled the car at a traffic light, but by the time she reached the Taconic Parkway she was driving with confidence. The parkway wound through green pastures and dark forests. Colored leaves still clung to many of the trees.

Passing the Hudson exits, she could not help thinking of Piet; he was just beyond the lavender hills on her right. She left the Taconic at the last exit and drove northward through little towns and open country, past farms and orchards. In Bennington, Vermont, she stopped for lunch and to walk the kinks out of her neck and back.

The Molly Stark Trail from Bennington to Brattleboro was worse than she remembered. Hairpin turns. Steep inclines after which the highway dropped so quickly that escape routes had been installed for runaway trucks. When the road finally flattened, Meg was breathing like a locomotive; her hands were sweaty. In Brattleboro, she turned north for a few miles and then left onto a narrow county road.

A sign at the side of the road caused her to slow almost to a stop: "Bowers, 6 Miles Ahead. Gas. Food. Lodging." *It was just a gas station,* she breathed. *Small and filthy.* But that was ten years ago. Of course she knew they'd made changes since they bought it.

Meg drove on, recognizing some of the older farmhouses and a silo that had been leaning like the tower of Pisa for as long as Meg could remember. And then she slowed again, pulled onto the shoulder, and gazed at overgrown land on her right. As if in a dream, she opened the car door and climbed out.

She walked back along the side of the road to the spot where the vegetable stand had once stood. Through the tangle of weeds, she could just make out the vestiges of the driveway. She headed toward the maple that had sheltered their trailer. When had the trailer been taken away? She sniffed the fragrant air; somewhere nearby someone was burning hickory logs in a fireplace or stove.

She pushed her way on through stickery underbrush until she came to the stream, just a trickle this time of the year. Suddenly she looked beyond the stream and joy swept her soul.

"You made it!" she shouted, spreading her arms and jumping down into the streambed, over the trickle and up on the opposite bank. She pushed aside mostly bare swaying branches and embraced the fat trunk of a weeping willow tree. "I never really forgot you," she whispered. She looked up through the few yellow leaves that still clung to the slender branches. "My, how you've grown!" She laughed aloud.

Meg dropped to the ground and sat with her back against the trunk of the tree. Many years ago, Peggy had played house under the parent of this tree. The owner of the old tree had cut twigs from it, which Meg had brought home and planted near the stream. She had watered the twigs faithfully for the rest of the summer. Fall came and they lost their leaves, of course. In the spring only one of them grew new leaves. She had watered it for several years, even after her mother had left. One day she had looked at it critically; it was growing too slowly to shelter her during her childhood. At the time she had felt betrayed. "But you kept right on growing, didn't you?" she said aloud.

Looking out through the branches to the other side of the stream, she saw the place where she had planted her first radishes. She felt a smile creep onto her face. There were some happy memories here. She had been born in Boston but her father had left his engineering job in the late sixties to become an organic farmer and live off the land. The vegetable stand was never a booming success, but her father had worked hard and many winters he'd had a job running ski lifts. Her mother had waited tables at a nearby inn. Meg had never before recognized that she and her mother had done exactly the same thing when they needed to earn money.

Meg was trying to resurrect more memories of the time before her mother had left, when the branches parted. "Hi, Peggy. Can I come in?" Her brother dropped down beside her.

She turned and studied him, raising her hands and smoothing the bushy eyebrows that met above the bridge of his nose. She remembered doing that to their father when he had come to kiss her good night. There was very little red left in Barry's dark brown, close-cropped hair. His eyes were small and gray, gentle like their father's eyes. He looked more like their father than ever, except that their father had been very tall and thin and Barry was very tall—almost as tall as Piet—and square. She put her hand on his. He covered it with his other hand. They sat silently for long minutes.

At last she asked the question that had haunted her for twenty years: "Why did Mama leave us? I got off the school bus and she wasn't waiting beside the road. She wasn't in the house. I never saw her again . . ."

"She did try to say good-bye to me because I was older. She was waiting for me in Hank's eighteen-wheeler when I came out of the high school that day. They were on their way to Florida. She said that the sun shone every day in Florida. Hank had promised to buy her a pretty red dress and they were going to go dancing and to the movies and swimming in the ocean. She was a silly, shallow woman, Peggy. She still is."

"You've seen her?" Meg was shocked.

"They've dropped by a couple of times."

"You didn't let them stay with you?"

"They came in a Winnebago and parked it behind the motel where we have a few hookups."

"Did you ever ask her why she didn't take us with her—or come back to visit us?"

"I ask but she always responds with a question: Why would we have wanted to go with her? Our schools and our home were here. We knew that she loved us. Didn't she tell us so on the postcards she sent faithfully on the first day of every month?"

"Are you able to forgive her, Barry?"

"I try."

"I try never to think of her. Everything was so miserable after she left."

"You've got the time frame skewed, Peggy. We got along all right the first couple of years after Mom left. I was a senior in high school when Dad's bronchitis got so bad he couldn't turn the soil. But the first years were okay. Don't forget that."

She had forgotten that. She'd thought that the welfare checks and food stamps had begun the same winter that Mama had gone away.

"So I was eleven when things got really bad, and you were eighteen." The significance of what she had said hit her like a fist below her ribs. "You were eighteen! You continued to work at the gas station. Did you want to go to college, Barry? Did you have to stay home to look out for me?"

"No, Peggy. I moved out. Remember? So that you and Dad could continue to collect welfare. I thought I wanted to go to college—to play football—but it wouldn't have done me much good. I was always better with my hands than with my brain. Besides, Barb was here. You have nothing to regret."

"Except that I was blind to your feelings and needs."

"You were a child. All children are self-centered, mine included."

"I'm looking forward to seeing your children, Barry."

Barry stood. "I'm glad you've come home, Peggy."

"How'd you know I was here?"

"Bud Dempster—remember him?—passed you when you were apparently reading our road sign. He recognized your Bower-colored hair. He mentioned it to me while he was filling his tank. When you didn't show up in a reasonable time, I began to worry about you. You might have had a flat. So I came looking and when I saw a car parked here . . ." He turned and stepped down into the streambed.

"Are you a substantial citizen, Barry?" she called.

"I'm a selectman and a deacon." He laughed and waved. "And you're a big-time lawyer. I guess we've shown the people of Brinton a thing or two."

She sat under her tree for a long time, laughing sometimes as she remembered "forgotten" pieces of her past. The treats her mother had brought home from the inn and placed on her pillow. Rainy days when she had dressed in her mother's "jewels" and high heels. The kitten her mother gave her.

None of these happy memories compensated for the fact that she had gone away without even saying good-bye. She still sent Meg cards at Christmas and on her birthday, sugary cards addressed to "my darling daughter." Meg did not respond. What was there to say?

Meg thought about her father and how he had read to her long after she could read to herself. He had told her stories. He had given her a section of the garden to be her own, and he told everyone that Peggy's vegetables were the best. The vegetarian food he cooked was boring, but it was nutritious. She couldn't remember that he had ever raised his voice to her. Peggy had loved her gentle, sweet-natured, bumbling father. Meg loved his memory.

After a time, she realized that dampness had

seeped through her corduroy jeans. She rose to her feet and patted her tree. "If I'm not back for a while, you have yourself a good winter."

She was getting into the car when she noticed a faded sign tacked to a tree near the road: Land For Sale.

She drove slowly toward town until she came to "Bowers," where she once again pulled off onto the shoulder to gaze with wonder at a large lawn with a small swimming pond in the center. Two rows of motel units met to form the back corner of the lawn. The gas station was where it had always been, at the intersection of a road that led to Putney and the road that led on into Brinton, but the walls were bright with fresh yellow paint. Looking beyond the pond to the Putney road, she half recognized a house. It had been dark green the last time she had seen it, with a refrigerator on the wraparound porch and tires scattered in the yard. Now it was yellow, with evergreens growing close to the porch. She smiled and drove on to park in front of a new building attached to the garage.

She stood for a moment in the doorway. Barb was pouring coffee for two businessmen sitting at the counter. She had changed very little. The brown hair that she had once worn long with bangs was pulled back into a smooth ponytail. She was the kind of trim little person that few people noticed until they were struck by her almost perfect features. Soft brown eyes, a small straight nose, a nicely shaped small mouth.

Meg's glance swept from the tables in front of the plant-filled windows overlooking the pond to the large round table in the center of the room where three children sat with their heads together. The girls were giggling; the boy looked away from them, disgusted. His eyes met Meg's and he jumped to his feet and ran toward her, stopping just beyond arm's reach. His sisters came and stood beside him. The youngest had straight red hair, just like Meg's had been at that age. One knee was skinned, the other was bruised.

Meg wanted to press all three of them to her in a giant bear hug. Instead, she took one step forward and smiled. She put her hands on the boy's shoulders. He was the proverbial string bean with a cowlick in his brown hair.

"Hello, John," she said. "I am so very glad to see you, to see all of you, and I am truly sorry that I did not come much sooner. You seem very tall for twelve. Are you?"

"I'm the tallest boy in my class except for Marvin and he's fourteen," John said proudly.

"He got all A's on his last report card," Katy said, tugging on Meg's jacket.

"Good for you." Meg kissed John on the cheek and turned to kiss the little girl. "And you're almost six, aren't you, Katy?"

"And I'm in kindergarten and I can read . . . a little. The doll you gave me for Christmas is my favorite doll. Her name is Margaret. Daddy says that's your real name. She's sleeping now but I'll let you hold her."

Meg ruffled the child's hair and turned to the middle child, who was also tall and, Meg thought, very pretty. "Happy birthday, Betsy. Your present is in the trunk of that little red car out there. Bring in the whole shopping bag, please." She kissed her and handed her the keys to the car.

Barb came out from behind the counter and stood in front of Meg, frowning. "You've made Barry and the children so happy," she whispered.

But I'm not making you happy, Meg thought. *Why?* "I'm glad to see them—and you. I should never have stayed away so long."

Barb shook her head sadly from side to side, and suddenly Meg understood. Barb wasn't ready to forgive Meg for neglecting the people Barb most loved.

"I'm sorry, Barb. I really am." She kissed her sister-in-law's cheek.

Barb smiled weakly and began to move slices of pies and cakes to the big round table. "We have dessert after school instead of after dinner," Barb explained.

A teenage girl presided at the counter while the Bower family gathered around the table. When they had finished eating, Meg handed a wrapped book to each child and a larger package to Betsy, who opened it to reveal a blue sweater that had caught Meg's eye as soon as she had entered the preteen department at Bloomingdale's. It was the color of the sky on a sunny day and the wool was as soft as a kitten's fur.

Betsy reached out one finger to touch it. "It's beautiful," she whispered, lifting it from the box and holding it in front of her. And then she ripped off her sweatshirt and pulled the sweater on over her head. It fit perfectly and Meg sighed with relief, glad that she had bought a size larger than the clerk had suggested. Betsy was going to be as tall as her Aunt Peggy. Betsy's other gift was a copy of *The Secret Garden.*

Barry and Meg were chatting about the enormous changes he and Barb had made to the gas station and the house, when Meg looked down to her left and saw that Katy was staring into her face. "Daddy says that I look like you," she whispered, shaking her head from side to side.

"That's because my hair was like yours when I was your age."

"The kids at school call me Carrotty. I don't like that."

"That's because they wish they had red hair."

"Your hair isn't red."

"It got darker. Yours will too, Katy. I promise."

The child grinned happily and for some reason she could not explain, Meg felt tears rising behind her eyes. She rose from the table and began clearing it.

When the tray was filled, Barry came and put his arm around her. "Why don't you drive your car over to the unit closest to the house?" He handed her a key. "Come to the house whenever you feel like it. We have dinner at six-thirty."

"But we don't get any dessert," Katy added.

As she parked in front of the motel unit, Meg noticed that there were cars in front of only two other units. There would be few tourists now until the ski season opened. Her room was simply furnished and sparkling clean. She dropped her bag, pulled back the spread, and lay on the bed with her hands behind her head and thought about the five people who were her family. She loved each one of them. She jumped up from the bed, washed her face, and ran to join them. After dinner she and the children sat on the floor in front of the fireplace and played Parcheesi.

She slept soundly straight through the night and on into the morning. The family had already eaten when Meg poured herself a mug of coffee and sat down at the counter of the coffee shop. Barb put a glass of juice and a plate of toast in front of her.

"What time did you begin work?" Meg asked Barb.

"Six-thirty. We open at seven."

"How late do you stay open?"

"At five the girl you saw here yesterday closes the coffee shop, makes a fresh pot of coffee and puts it and whatever pastries are left over on the counter there. People wait on themselves. A young man pumps gas until nine, when he unplugs the coffeepot and locks the station."

Meg took a bite of the toast and grinned at Barb. "Best I ever ate. Nutty. Did you bake it, Barb?"

"Yes, it's the sunflower seeds."

"You bake the pastries, too?"

She nodded. "I like to bake."

"But, my gosh, Barb, you work here from six-thirty and then you go home and care for your house and your children."

"Don't worry about me. I have help now so that I can take time off during the day. We're closed Sundays except during the high tourist seasons. We used to work sixteen hours a day but now—"

"You don't have to work like that anymore. Oh, Barb, I am so glad for you and I am so glad that I came back yesterday. And . . ." Unable to say all that was in her heart, she spread her hands helplessly.

"It *is* Peggy Bower. I just couldn't believe. Not after all these years." A woman, who reeked of cloying perfume, hugged her from the back. "You won't remember me, not now that you've become a famous lawyer." The woman leaned around Meg to give her a chance to prove her memory. She was plump, with Cupid's bow lips turned into a prim smile.

"Coffee, Sharon?" Barb asked quickly.

Meg reached across the counter and tapped her sister-in-law's hand to thank her for rescuing her. "Sharon Davis." Meg smiled falsely.

"Sharon Johnson, but I wouldn't expect you to know that. I married Al Johnson."

"Do you have children?" Meg asked, for want of anything else to say.

"Two. Boy first and then a girl. You, of course, haven't had time for children. You haven't even had time to come back to visit your brother and all your old friends. Why'd you come now?"

"I wanted to see my brother and Barb and the children." Suddenly Meg remembered one other person she wanted to see. "I'd also like to see Miss Mills. Is she still in town?"

"Dear Miss Mills. She was kind to you, as I recall. Got you that scholarship to Smith, though I never could understand why you had to go to a fancy school like that. You always did think you were better . . . Oh dear. I mustn't say anything unkind. Not even if I am one of your oldest friends. Tell me. Do you like living in New York City? I hear the homeless are lying in every doorway. And the crime! I suppose you're used to being robbed and mugged." She leaned forward to whisper in Meg's ear. "Have you been raped?"

"Sorry to disappoint you, Sharon, but I have never been accosted by anyone more evil than a rather polite beggar." Meg rose from the counter. "I told John I'd help him stack wood this morning. Good to have seen you, Sharon."

She was almost to the wood pile near the house when she realized that she had not lied to Sharon. It had been good *for Meg* to see the tactless woman whom she had allowed to become a motivating force in her life. She and John stacked wood until noon.

After lunch, Meg walked through town in a tweed suit and low-heeled pumps, greeting people who greeted her, whether she could remember them or not. She had forgotten that Brinton was a pretty little town with its clapboard houses and shops.

Meg had phoned ahead, so Miss Mills was expecting her. Although she had retired eight years earlier, she was still arrow straight and her voice was still her most attractive feature. Meg had written a few letters to this favorite English teacher who had not only encouraged her to apply for a scholarship to Smith but who had also found her the job on the Cape. She thanked her, once again, and they chatted amiably.

"I sense a certain reserve when you discuss your work, Peggy. Is there something displeasing about your firm in New York, or about the work you do? I understand that major law firms pay very well."

"Indeed they do. I make a salary so large it

shocks even me. Of course I still have school debts and I am expected to dress well. The firm is old and prestigious. The people I work with are bright, honest, generally pleasant. It's me I'm having problems with. I work at least sixty hours a week and much of what I do is tedious. There are so many of us working on every project that I seldom feel that *I* have accomplished anything. I don't think that I like living in the city, either. Coming back here has made me even more aware of what a country mouse I am." She told Miss Mills about the willow tree. "Ten years ago I promised myself I would never live in a small town again."

"Adolescent promises are not always to be trusted."

"True." Meg laughed. "And my life is far from grim; I have several options. I could work in the city and live in the suburbs. I could live and work in the city and eventually buy myself a weekend cottage in the country. I could leave the city and set up a private practice in the country, perhaps in Brattleboro."

"Would small-town kinds of cases interest you, Peggy?"

Meg thought a moment and then nodded. "They would involve people as opposed to corporations and I could see most of them through on my own. I could also refuse work I didn't want to handle." She giggled. "Maybe I could be a plant lawyer. I might represent the dandelion in a libel suit against the general populace. 'My client is not a pest but an eager bloomer who makes dull green lawns sparkle with yellow and puffs of white.' "

Miss Mills laughed. "And what could a lawyer say on behalf of poison ivy?"

Meg thought a moment. "We'd plead self-defense. 'My client didn't want to harm the victim who was crushing my client underfoot and pulling his roots from the earth.' "

Before dinner, Barry asked his sister to come outside with him. He led her to the back of the property and pushed aside the branches of a red-leafed Japanese maple to show her a simple bronze plaque: John Bower, 1930 to 1984.

Soon after she had graduated from high school, her father had moved into a commune in New York State. Although she had invited him to visit her at Smith, he had never come. He wrote infrequently. During the summer after her junior year, he died.

"There was a service for him at the commune. You didn't have a service here, did you?"

"No, we're not sure it's legal to bury ashes on private property so Barb read the twenty-third psalm and I said a prayer."

"I walked for hours on the beach after you called. I was furious with Daddy for getting sick, for not coming to see me, and for dying. At the same time I felt terrible because I had never told him that he was a loving, kind father. I should have come here at the time."

"You're here now." Barry patted her shoulder and walked back to the house.

Meg dropped to her knees and pulled a clump of grass from the base of the little tree. "I loved you, Daddy," she whispered.

* * *

That night Meg thought about a story her father had often told her. It was called "The Three Sillies." Meg now knew three other sillies: her mother, Sharon Davis, and Meg herself. *These three and the greatest is me.* Meg couldn't let that rhyme stand. *These three and the greatest fool is I.*

Chapter Seventeen

AFTER church and lunch on Sunday, Meg said good-bye to her family, promising to come back for Thanksgiving. She was already in the car when Barb laid a bag on the front passenger seat. "Just a few pastries and rolls," she said. "Please don't disappoint them on Thanksgiving, Peggy."

"I'll be here, Barb. That's a promise. Nothing less than two broken legs or a six-foot snow storm could keep me away."

A fine mist clouded the windshield as she drove out of Brinton. It had turned to rain by the time she reached Brattleboro. Reluctant to drive the treacherous Molly Stark Trail to Bennington in the rain, Meg pulled to the side of the road to study her map and then went straight south on U.S. 91. From there she could either turn west on the Mass Pike, or she could stay on 91 south into Connecticut and turn west when she was almost to Peekskill.

The former route would take her within a mile or two of Stonefield. She could stop—for just a few minutes—to tell Piet about her fabulous family and about the willow tree that had kept on growing. And then he would take her in his arms. What she imagined was so delicious that she shivered.

What if he did not take her in his arms? What if the divorcée had moved into the A-frame? Meg swerved dangerously close to the shoulder and gave her full attention to the slick highway. She did not turn off at the Mass Pike.

On the train from Peekskill to New York she considered opening a law office in Brattleboro. She would have to pass the Vermont bar exam, which was more difficult than most bar exams. She would have to find an office. She couldn't help thinking of the mustard-colored house in Stonefield. Maybe she could find something like that with an office downstairs and living quarters above. Eventually, maybe she could buy the land with her willow tree and have a little house built for herself. In the meantime, she would have to find a way to support herself while she was getting established. Would she have to wait tables again—and depend on tips? She shook her head. Returning to Vermont would be a giant step backward.

During the following week, she concentrated on her work. Over a period of ten years she had developed a single-track mind that had kept her chugging along toward success. Although she was beginning to doubt that she had defined success correctly, she stuck to her old habits, reminding herself that the money that came from success could buy educations for her nieces and nephew, presents for her family, and food and shelter for a few of the needy.

When she thought about Piet, and she thought of him too often, she reminded herself that he was Rick's brother, perhaps the divorcée's boyfriend, and a man whose life-style was drastically different from her own. Furthermore, she hardly knew him. What she felt for him was nothing more than lust. The word "lust" electrified her body with the passion she had felt on the afternoon of the storm.

On the Sunday after her return from Brinton, Rick called and invited her to have dinner with him. She declined. "A drink, then? I've got to see you, Meg."

"I'd rather not, Rick."

"I have a message from Aunt Hat." His voice was teasing.

"So tell me over the phone. My line's not tapped."

"Nope. You want to hear what she said, you'll have to meet me at Dino's in an hour." He hung up, knowing he had won.

He was waiting at a table when she arrived and he stood, smiling broadly, and kissed her on the cheek, holding her close until she pulled away. He ordered the draft beer she liked and, as soon as they had tapped their glasses, he told her Miss Pearce's message.

"She said you were the best houseguest she's had in twenty years and she hopes you'll be back soon. She also said that she thought you might have done me a lot of good. Want to give it another try, Meg?" He asked the question casually, as if it didn't matter much one way or the other.

Meg laughed. "No, Rick, I don't want to give it another try. But thanks for the invite."

"So how are things at the three S's?"

"Fine. I'm still in the tax department."

"Don't you miss the Dixon folk?"

"How do you know?" She paused. "Of course. They filed weeks ago. Everyone knows they're trying to get control of Smengines."

"Are they going to be successful?"

"I haven't any idea, Rick. I haven't even thought of them for weeks."

"You don't see your old friends in mergers and acquisitions? Joel, for instance."

Meg was beginning to feel wary. "I see them but we haven't discussed this client and I wouldn't tell you if we had."

Rick reached across the table and grabbed her wrist, holding it tightly. "So find out what's going on. That's all I ask."

Meg stared at him and then it all came clear. "You bought Smengines stock," she breathed.

"Right. It's more than doubled in four months. But I heard a rumor last week that makes me wonder . . . Should I sell out on Monday or wait for it to triple?"

Meg rose to her feet. "I can't believe that you would put me in this position."

"What position? You didn't tell me to buy. It's not your fault—or to your credit—that I put two and two together. It was a once-in-a-lifetime opportunity and I seized it. The early worm and all that."

She turned away from the table and stumbled toward the door and out onto the sidewalk. She had gone half a block when he caught up with her.

"Get off your high horse, Meg, and tell me why you're so angry."

"You know about insider trading. We even discussed it, as I recall."

"Sure, I know about insider trading. What you fail to remember is that I am not an insider. If either company were my client, there might be a problem, but they are not."

"But Dixon was my client and I was engaged to you. Is that why you sold your land to Piet? So you'd have money to buy stock you heard about at a party you attended as my fiancé?"

"No problem. We're not engaged now. But for old times' sake, just find out how things are going. All I want you to tell me is this: will the price go higher? I'll phone you tomorrow—"

"I will not accept your call, Rick." She hurried on ahead of him.

"Please, Meg, just this one favor."

She increased her speed.

"I saw Piet this weekend," he called.

Meg wanted to keep walking but her feet seemed to be embedded in the sidewalk cement.

He took her arm and pushed her away from the crowds on Third Avenue into a recessed doorway. "He was getting ready for a party with a bunch of the local yokels. They're his type."

"Jerry and Laura may be locals but they are definitely not yokels," Meg said angrily.

"Point taken, but may I remind you that you have not met all of Piet's friends? It's like I told

Silly Sally—that's what I called the girl he was about to marry—Piet is a sweet simple soul, boring to people with get-up-and-go. I advised her to get out while the going was easy."

"*You* advised your brother's girl to dump him, two days before the wedding?"

"I met her for the first time a week before the wedding. She was a pretty little thing and had been at U. Mass for two years. I 'seen my duty and I done it.' " He laughed while Meg stared at him in horror. "Little did I know she was going to come looking for me. She transferred to NYU—I was at Columbia at the time—and made a real nuisance of herself—"

"Because you had led her on." Meg's voice trembled, her face felt flushed.

"I took her out a couple of times."

"Big of you." Meg sneered. "What happened to Sally? Does Piet know what you did?"

"Piet doesn't even suspect. I've thought of telling him. He should be grateful. She'd have been dissatisfied with him before their first anniversary. Besides, Miss Sally was incredibly tactless. When she broke the engagement, she told Piet she'd met someone else who was more sophisticated and better educated, et cetera, et cetera. She got her just reward. I ran into her on Fifth Avenue a couple of years ago. Living in New Jersey with a high school teacher husband and a bunch of brats. She's overweight and dowdy."

Meg felt dizzy with rage. "You're a snake, Rick, deceitful, arrogant, manipulative—"

"You're very attractive with the green lights flashing in your eyes, Meg."

Did he think that line was original? Meg pushed him aside and stomped out onto the sidewalk.

"Not everyone agrees with you, my dear," he called after her. "I'll probably ask Jocelyn to marry me. She's much more pliable than you are."

And wealthier, Meg thought.

"It'll be the society event of the season. We'll send you an invitation—if you give me the information I want. I'll call you tomorrow."

For a while after she returned to her apartment, Meg was so angry with Rick that she couldn't think of anything but his treachery. Finally she asked herself if it was her duty to tell Mr. Spencer about Rick's stock purchase. No, the real sinner had been the associate who had mentioned the matter at the partner's picnic. He was no longer with the firm.

She let her thoughts move from Rick to herself. She was one lousy judge of people. She had undervalued her brother and her father. She had misjudged herself when she had chosen corporate law. She had loved Rick, never suspecting that he was a traitor. Meg Bower was, in short, a fool.

Had she misjudged Piet, too? She had believed him when he said he loved her. Was it possible that she, Meg, was merely a challenge to Piet? Had it amused him to chase his brother's girlfriend? Maybe he did know about Rick's betrayal. Maybe he had used her to seek revenge.

No, no, no, no. She had to believe that Piet was sincere. He would never suspect his brother of such perfidy. Meg would like to be the person to set him straight. She composed a speech in her head: *I hate to tell you this, Piet, but you really should know* . . . That was a speech she would *never* deliver; it would hurt Piet too much.

At least she understood why Piet made disparaging remarks about himself. She wondered if Silly Sally had pretended to love the gardens; is that why Piet had accused Meg of putting on an act?

During the week, Rick called her at home. She hung up. He left messages for her at her office and on her answering machine. She never returned his calls.

When her phone rang late the following Sunday night she waited for the machine to pick it up and then she gasped. It was Piet! She intercepted the call with a breathless, "Hello, Piet."

He didn't bother with "Hello" and "How are you?" but launched right in. "Fred was here this afternoon. Seems he's very angry with you, accusing you of blocking him somehow. I don't know what he's talking about, but I've thought it over and I can't believe that you're at fault, Meg. If there's some way I can help you. . . ."

She shook her head and then realized that he couldn't see her silent denial. "No, Piet. There's no problem. Rick wants me to tell him if he should sell some stock or wait for it to go higher. The information I might obtain is privileged; I can't tell him. That's all there is to it. It was nice of you to offer to help, Piet. I really appreciate this call."

"How are you, Meg?"

"Fine, I guess. And you? Rick said you'd been dating an attractive divorcée." She bit her tongue. *How could she say anything so dumb?*

"You believed him, of course. Why not?" Piet's words scorched her ear.

"I'm sorry, Piet. Please forgive—"

Piet cut the line between them.

Meg beat her fist into her pillow.

The only happy thing Meg could think of was Thanksgiving with Barry and family. She worked like a cold, efficient robot all day and far into the night. She took more driving lessons and reserved a car for the long weekend.

She also went for walks and read the catalogs that were now featuring Christmas gifts for the gardener. She received subscription offers from *Horticulture* and *Organic Gardening*. Even as she was thinking how stupid it was for a gardening company to send expensive mailings to an address in Manhattan, she wrote a check for a two-year subscription to *Fine Gardening*.

Occasionally she considered opening a law practice in Brattleboro and buying the land with her weeping willow tree. Miss Pearce seemed happy living alone. Meg's life could be similar but better. She would have her work and her nieces and nephew.

She tried never to think of the brothers Graaf. Both were symbols of her inadequacy as a judge of people. She had regarded them as honorable men. Rick had lied to her and had taken advantage of information he received as her fiancé. When she thought of Rick she was furious. As for Piet, she had believed him when he said he loved her. Now she had moments when she still believed him—

and moments when she did not. She mourned when she thought of Piet.

There was another person whom she thought of often. That was Prudence. *No news is good news* she quoted to herself. Finally, with Mr. Spencer's permission, she phoned the director of the Lenox school.

"She's doing well academically and we've given her a job in the greenhouse, which she seems to enjoy, but she is still very fragile emotionally."

"Where will she be at Thanksgiving?" Meg asked.

"Here. She's not strong enough to go home yet. But don't worry, about half of our students will be here and we'll eat all of the traditional food. Pru is in charge of the table decorations."

"Could I visit her on my way back to the city from Vermont on the Saturday after Thanksgiving?" Meg asked.

The director assured her that she would be welcome.

Meg doubted that. Why should Prudence want to see her? Why, for that matter, should she want to see Prudence? *Because I have learned something I want to share with her*, Meg acknowledged.

Meg drove all the way from Manhattan to Brinton, arriving just in time to go with the family to Barb's parents' farmhouse for a Thanksgiving like none Meg had ever experienced. The diners, who ranged in age from Barb's one-month-old niece to her ninety-two-year-old great-aunt, sat at tables in the living room, the dining room, and the kitchen. The food was traditional, delicious, and plentiful. Meg wondered if Piet and Miss Pearce were eating Thanksgiving dinner alone. Perhaps the divorcée was with them. Meg dismissed them from her mind and spooned more dressing onto her plate.

After dinner Meg sat on the front porch with one of Barb's uncles, a lawyer in Brattleboro who assured her that the town needed another lawyer, two having retired within the last year. "Our cases may seem pretty trivial to a city lawyer, and so will our earnings," he warned her. "Actually, I'm thinking of slowing down, so if you want to leave the bright lights, give me a call and we'll talk." He handed her his business card.

Could it be that easy? she asked herself. *Could she just walk into another man's office and begin to take over his clients? Probably not.*

Chapter Eighteen

As Meg explained to her brother, driving into Manhattan on the Sunday after Thanksgiving would be too challenging for a fledgling city driver. Therefore, having obtained Christmas wish lists from each of the children, Meg drove down to Lenox on Saturday.

Prudence was not welcoming but she consented to show Meg the greenhouse and her room. When Meg walked over to the terrarium, Prudence explained that when she got it the gloxinia had been blooming.

"I called the man who delivered it to me. He said it was probably just resting but if it isn't budding again by Christmas, he'll come look at it." She paused and then leaned toward Meg. "Sometimes I hope it won't bud. He's a hunk."

Meg was at a loss to know how to respond. If she said she knew Piet, that would be proof that she, not Pru's father, had ordered the terrarium. Still, to deny knowing him was a lie.

Prudence solved the dilemma. "But you know

him. You ordered the terrarium, not dear old dad. I like it—and the hunk."

"Piet Graaf is a hunk. He's also an artist, and a nice person." Meg hesitated. "I'd like to share something with you, Prudence. We could go for a walk . . ."

"Ho-hum. Another lecture." The girl yawned dramatically and plopped down on her bed. "You can sit on my roommate's bed, but don't get comfortable; I can't stand long lectures."

Feeling less than encouraged, Meg sat on the edge of the bed and launched into her opening argument. "I want to talk to you about people who disappoint us and what we do in response to that disappointment."

Prudence rolled over so that her back was turned toward Meg.

"My mother left my father and brother and me when I was seven. She didn't say good-bye. She just drove off to Florida with a truck driver. All that year, every time I got off the school bus, I hoped she had come back. But she never did."

"You never saw her again?" Prudence muttered.

"Never. But she sent postcards and she still sends me Christmas cards and birthday cards."

"Big deal." Prudence turned over and looked at Meg.

"But my father was a good man; he loved me. The problem was that the people in town felt sorry for me and then my father got sick and we had to go on welfare and they pitied me even more and I couldn't stand it."

"So you started taking drugs, I suppose. What? A little grass? And then you saw the light . . ."

Ignoring the girl's mockery, Meg plunged on. "Just the opposite. I decided that I had to show everyone in town that I was the extreme opposite of pitiable. Whatever was best, that's what I had to have. The best college, the highest-paying profession, the highest position in that profession. I slaved to be the best, just so I could show the people in town that I was not a person to pity. In the meantime, I ignored my brother, who is a very nice man, and his children, whom I love dearly. I never asked myself if all of my splendid achievements were going to make me happy."

"Do they make you happy, Miz Big-time Lawyer?" Prudence asked, raising her head onto her hand.

"No. I find that I'm not happy in a big law office in a big city. But I'm not telling you this so that I'll have another person to pity me. I'm telling you because I think you're doing the same thing I've been doing. You're reacting to other people's expectations by hurling yourself in the opposite direction. I'll bet that if your father expected you to appear at a social function in a velvet dress with a lace collar, you'd wear torn jeans and a tie-dyed T-shirt. Just to show him."

Prudence shook her head. "I wore what he wanted me to wear for a long, long time. I did what he wanted me to do. It wasn't any use . . . Besides, I don't give a damn what he wants. Not anymore."

"So why don't you stop reacting to him and concentrate on what will make you happy? I can't believe it's drugs or gutter language."

"What do you think it might be, Miz Lady Lawyer?"

"I don't know, Prudence. What do you think? Plants, maybe?"

"I don't think anything except that I wish you'd leave me alone."

"Okay, Prudence. I've said what I had to say. Good-bye. Thank you for showing me the greenhouse and your terrarium." Meg walked to the door.

"You ever going to talk with your mother?" Prudence asked.

"I doubt it, but I might send her a card this Christmas."

"Good idea. Why don't you stuff the envelope with manure?" The girl laughed shrilly.

The word "manure" was an enormous improvement over the word Prudence would have used just two months earlier.

Having articulated her feelings about her work to Prudence, Meg was anxious to resign from the firm. On Monday she made an appointment to see Mr. Spencer. She told him she had visited Prudence, whose speech had improved if her demeanor had not. "But that's not why I made this appointment. I'm here to tell you that I made a mistake when I joined the firm and—"

"You'd go to another firm?" Mr. Spencer squinted at her over his half-glasses. "How much are they offering you?"

"I've felt privileged to be with Savage, Smith, and Spencer, and it would never occur to me to go elsewhere in Manhattan. My mistake was in thinking that I was cut out for a large corporate firm, any large corporate firm, in a large impersonal city, any large impersonal city. I will stay as long as necessary to provide for a smooth transition."

"So what are you going to do, if I may ask?" Suddenly Mr. Spencer leaned back in his big chair and smiled at her benignly. "You're going to get married. That's the trouble with women lawyers, though I must say that most of them wait until they have a child to quit or slow down. Does the young man live in another part of the country?"

"No, Mr. Spencer, I'm not planning to get married. I'm leaving to become a country lawyer, probably in Vermont."

"I cannot believe it. There is too much for you here. Why would you throw it over? Let me know if you change your mind—anytime before the end of the year."

Mr. Spencer was not the only person to challenge Meg's decision. Joel set up a luncheon with Meg and four other third-year associates, all of whom were her friends. As soon as they had ordered, he launched into the purpose of the meeting. "We care about you, Meg," he said. "We can't bear to see you make this disastrous mistake."

A woman sitting beside her took her hand. "We know you were engaged and that the engagement has been broken. That has to have been devastating. But you'll begin to feel better. It would be foolish to make a rash decision when—"

Meg grinned into the face of her sober friend. "Sorry to disappoint you, but I am not devastated by my broken engagement. Actually, I am relieved. I have made this decision because I am a country mouse and the things I value are not in New York City or at a large law firm."

"You enjoyed trusts," one of the men said. "Why don't you just stick around until there's a permanent opening there?"

"There are wills to be written in Vermont," Meg said.

The other woman at the table reminded Meg of her duty to women in general and women lawyers in particular. "Think of your position historically and accept your duty to carry the torch for the sisterhood."

Joel talked about the enormity of her investment and the magnitude of the reward that was waiting just a few years down the road.

The lawyers were, of course, articulate and they presented their arguments well. Meg's talents would be wasted. She would be bored away from the cultural attractions of the city. She could be a part-time country mouse and maintain her position at the three S's . . .

At the end of the meal, Meg thanked them for caring and promised to consider what they had said. She did not tell them that none of their arguments had moved her.

Meg's colleagues treated her as if she were either a balky child or a candidate for an insane asylum. Not one could understand her choice. It didn't matter to Meg. She rejoiced in the prospect of leaving her job and the city behind her. Each day she told herself that she would phone Barb's lawyer uncle in Brattleboro to set up an interview during the Christmas holidays.

* * *

In the meantime, 'twas the season to be jolly. If it were not for her longing to see Piet, Meg would have been entirely in harmony with the season.

Early in December, Jane called. "Is everything okay with you, Meg?" she asked. "Are you working and sleeping well? Do you have plans for the holidays?"

"Yes, to all three questions, Miz Shrink. I'm going to spend Christmas with my family in Brinton, Vermont. You didn't know I have a family, did you?"

"As a matter of fact, I did. I met your brother at graduation. A big man with hair the color of yours."

"I wish you'd had a chance to meet my father, too. He was a lovely and loving man. My brother owns a substantial business. He's a deacon in the church and a selectman. I never really appreciated his wife until . . . And the children are so wonderful." She rattled on about the virtues of each one of her nieces and her nephew until she suddenly laughed. "I sound just like Amy—remember her?—when she talks about her baby, who really is almost as adorable as she thinks he is."

Jane laughed. "I was worried about you, Meg, but I see I can cross you off my list of potential clients. Have a merry Christmas."

"I will because I will be with my family." Meg loved to say those two words: "my family." "And you, too." They went on to discuss Jane's plans.

A few days later, Amy called to invite Meg to join them for the holidays. Once again Meg could talk about her own wonderful family and her plans to leave the city.

"I was afraid you might be feeling sad—broken engagement and all."

She thanked Amy for caring and assured her that she was not sad, which was true. She was happy, when she was able to forget Piet.

Never before had she so enjoyed Christmas shopping. The children were the easiest because she had their lists. She bought each of them an item from the list and then she went to a large Fifth Avenue bookstore. On her way to the children's department, she passed a counter filled with art books. One seemed to jump up and say, "Buy me." She turned a few pages—the reproductions were lovely—and put it back on the counter. She didn't want a book on Hudson River paintings to lie around reminding her of a day she had best forget.

Eventually she found the right book for each of the girls and a group of paperback sports novels for John. The line at the register was long and so was the wait. As she neared the register she suddenly stepped out of line, picked up the book on Hudson River paintings, and repositioned herself at the end of the line for another long wait, all the time telling herself how silly she was. Several times she decided to leave the art book at the desk. With tax, it would cost over forty dollars. She didn't want it anyway. For reasons she could not understand, she bought the book and took it home and hid it in the closet.

On the Thursday evening when she shopped for Barry and Barb, she was joyfully extravagant. She bought Barry a heavy wool sweater and Barb a teal blue velour robe.

The next weekend she went in search of a "little something" for Miss Mills. At Lord and Taylor she was choosing between two wool challis scarves—both equally soft and colorful—when she decided to buy them both. She would mail one to Miss Pearce.

She reserved a car for the Saturday before Christmas, but she did not phone the lawyer in Brattleboro. *Tomorrow*, she kept promising herself. Nor did she mail the scarf to Miss Pearce.

When she had not called Brattleboro by Friday, December 20, she asked herself why. A wee voice whispered the answer: *You don't want to practice law in Brattleboro; you want to go to Stonefield. You want to deliver Miss Pearce's scarf yourself.*

That's dumb, she told the voice. The mustard-colored office had been sold. Piet wanted her to stay away. Why would she want to return to Stonefield? Because Miss Pearce was there, and her secret garden. Rick would also be there from time to time, which made no difference one way or the other. She could meet him on the street without any feeling beyond dismay at her own gullibility and his duplicity.

And Piet? Would she be able to greet him naturally? No. So she should stay away, shouldn't she? Rick had wounded his brother a long time ago. Was it possible that Meg could kiss the hurt and make it go away? Could she convince him that Rick and her education and her salary—soon she'd have no salary—need not be barriers to a future relationship. What about the divorcée? Was she part of Piet's life or just someone he had coffee with once? If only she and Piet could talk frankly to one another, if they could get to know one another better. That's all she wanted, she told herself.

Meg picked up the phone and dialed Piet's number. "Hello," he said, and her heart swung from the high wire to the sawdust below.

"Hello, Piet." Her voice trembled. "Hello, Piet. I've called to ask you a simple question." She held the phone away from her and looked at it. "But not on the phone," she whispered and hung up.

Chapter Nineteen

SHE awoke at five, showered and forced herself to eat a bowl of cereal. She was dressed and her bags were lined up beside the door long before the office, where she had reserved a car, had opened.

She couldn't sit still in her own room. Her body felt as if it were being stretched on the rack; she was nauseous. She dreaded the drive. She dreaded meeting Piet. He might be angry with her for knocking on his door. How would he show it? Would he be icy formal or boiling angry? She'd glimpsed his temper; she didn't know enough about him to know if it was ever uncontrollable. She didn't know much about Piet except that he was passionate and . . .

"Enough," she said aloud as she headed for the door. She'd wait on the doorstep of the rental office.

The sky, which is never truly black in New York City, was turning a lighter gray when she stepped out of her building. The first car parked beyond the bus stop was a little blue Ford, a nice car to rent. The next car was a black Mercedes. She wondered if one day she might rent a Mercedes, not this time, but sometime. *A black Mercedes, an old black Mercedes, with Massachusetts plates!*

She ran to it, and leaned down to peer into the window from the sidewalk. Piet sat behind the wheel, his head against the rest, sleeping. Tears rose in her eyes as she stood looking at him. It wasn't just his physical beauty, though he was, indeed, a very handsome man. He was strong, and good, and honest; those were absolutes that she suddenly accepted with no cloud of doubt. She desired him, oh how she desired him! She also admired him. She loved him. And he was here, parked in front of her building.

She tapped on the window and watched, enchanted, as he turned his head toward her. He opened his eyes, squinted, and beamed brilliantly, like the rising sun. His movements seemed to be in slow motion. Leaning toward her, he unlocked the door and pushed it open. He took her hand as she slid into the passenger seat and pulled her into his arms and kissed her slowly. It was as if he were savoring her presence.

He kissed her more urgently; she responded. Suddenly he stopped and eased her back against the curbside door, while he leaned against the opposite door and crossed his arms in front of his chest. "I've come because I have something to say to you. I said I loved you, Meg."

"Don't you love me, Piet?" she asked. It was an inane question. Of course he loved her; she was sure of that.

"Oh yes, Meg, I love you. Every day I love you more. We're not well matched. So what? Contrasts are interesting. I'm going to do my damnedest to convince you of that."

"I don't think it will take much—"

"Let me finish. It's taken me all fall to realize what a selfish fool I've been, expecting you to give up your position here to move to Stonefield to be with me. I do have an obligation to Miss Pearce and the arboretum and my clients. It's seasonal. In the winter, I can hire someone to run the snow blower and I can whittle in a skyscraper just as well as in my A-frame."

When Meg opened her mouth to speak, Piet put his finger across it.

"So here's what I propose: We can spend six months of the year here in the city or some convenient place near the city. During the other six months we can be together on weekends and during your vacation. Please, Meg, forgive me for not seeing how selfish I was being, for thinking you'd want to practice law in that little office. I'll rent it out, if you'll—"

"My turn." She leaned forward and put her finger across his lips and rested her head on his shoulder. "You may have noticed that it is very early in the morning? 'Where could Meg be going?' You might have asked yourself that, if you'd been thinking clearly."

"Right. Where are you going at . . ." He straightened his arm and looked at his watch over her shoulder. "At six forty-five on a Saturday morning?"

"To pick up a car to drive to Brinton with a stopover in Stonefield to see you. I have quit my job. I think I'd like to move to Stonefield if you and I . . . If we could . . . I want us to have a chance to get to know one another."

"You didn't have to quit your job. If you think we need more time to date in a conventional sort of way, I could come down weekends and court you. I'd love to court you, Meg. I'll bring you chocolates and flowers and take you to fancy restaurants and the theater. Incidentally, in case you think I am poor, I am not. I don't make nearly as much as you make, but my living expenses are not so great and I have no debts. I'm comfortable."

"And you love what you do."

"That's true."

"I left my law firm because I didn't like the work I was doing, or living in the city. I need to live among trees and flowers and my kind of people, people like my brother—and you, Piet. It's time for me to acknowledge that." She lifted his hand and kissed it. "I have to tell you about my brother and his family in Brinton. I cut myself off from them—and missed so much—because I was a fool. I have lots to tell you about them and me. It will take all day."

"It just so happens that I have all day, a lifetime, in fact, to hear whatever you have to say. You say you planned to rent a car. So what shall we do about that?"

While they were walking to the car rental office to cancel Meg's reservation, she asked him how long he'd been parked in front of her building.

"Couple of hours. I've been wanting to talk to you for a long, long time. And then last night you phoned and I knew you were right; we couldn't talk on the phone. So I went to bed and I woke up at one-thirty and left a note for Miss Pearce and took the Mercedes. I've been here since about four-thirty." Suddenly, he spun himself around a lamppost and kissed her on the nose.

On the way from the office to her apartment to pick up her bags, she asked him what he meant about the office in Stonefield. "It's been sold. I saw that when I was through there in October."

"To me. No one wanted it because it is on a lot only thirty feet wide. The town was deciding to buy it for a song, planning to raze the house to provide a few parking places. I bought it for barely more than a song, because I couldn't give up the dream that one day you would come back . . ." He grabbed her hand and brought it to his lips. "When everything between us seemed beyond hope, I decided to convert it to two small apartments, but I couldn't bring myself to even enter the place." Back in her room, he took her in his arms.

"It's lust," she whispered in his ear. "I've been asking myself this question: Is it lust or love I feel for Piet? That's one reason we should have a courtship. So that we can research the question."

He nodded thoughtfully. "Sounds like an important project." His arms tightened around her and then relaxed. "But we'd better not start now or we'll never make it to Stonefield."

She swallowed and agreed, reluctantly. He picked up her bags while she went to her closet and lifted the Hudson River painting book from the shelf. God must have known she would need a Christmas gift for Piet.

Before they drove off, he turned to her. "This research project could take years, you know. Don't you think we could marry on the basis of a few preliminary findings, and then pursue the research at leisure?"

"That's a sensible suggestion, Piet. It may take a lifetime to arrive at the definitive answer."

"That's if we're diligent and work at it every day." He grinned at her and turned the key in the ignition.

Traffic was so light that Meg could begin to tell Piet about her family, past and present, as they drove through the city toward the Taconic Parkway. When they stopped for breakfast in Westchester, she phoned Barb to say that she would not be in Brinton for several days. She'd call again to tell her exactly when she would arrive. She hoped to bring someone with her, if that was okay.

Barb laughed. "I'm completely confused, Peggy, but I think I am very happy for you."

Meg reported that sentence as they drove out of the parking lot. "You'll like my family," she said. "Just wait until you meet my nieces and nephew. And my brother is a wonderful person."

"My brother has not been a wonderful person, Meg, but I'm grateful to him for bringing you to Stonefield."

Your brother is a despicable, disloyal louse. That's what Meg wanted to say. "I'm grateful too, Piet. Rick is an attractive, ambitious, charming man—"

Piet braked and turned the car onto a ramp leading to an overlook where he parked. The face he turned toward Meg was distraught. "And?" he asked anxiously.

"*But* I do not like him very much, *and* I could be alone with him in a shed in the rain for the rest of my life and not want to touch him."

Piet held her close, whispering her name over and over.

As they drove on toward Stonefield, Meg told him what she had told Prudence. "I was trying to make myself into something I am not. I was compelled to prove how terrific I am to myself and to people I thought pitied me. The important thing for you to understand, Piet, is that the person who was engaged to Rick was not the real me."

When they had been on the road for more than two hours—it seemed like two minutes—she came to a sudden halt in her narrative.

"There, I've brought you up to date. Now tell me about you."

"There's not much to tell. I've done a lot of carving this fall. About the woman you called the divorcée. . . ."

"You don't have to tell me, Piet."

"I want to. She and I have been friends since we were teenagers. In fact, I took her to the senior prom, because neither of us had a date. She married a rotter who left her with a mortgage and three little kids. I'm still her friend, so I've had coffee with her a couple of times and let her cry on my shoulder. I patched her roof, too. It made me mad to think that you would even suspect that I would look at anyone but you. Then I realized that Fred wanted you to think she was someone I was involved with romantically."

"I had a couple of dates." Meg told him about the politician. "In retrospect, I can see that he was a lot like Rick. Both men want women who will be assets to their careers. Rick never introduced me to anyone without dragging Smith and Harvard and the law firm into the conversation. He's irrational in that respect. The president of his company has a wife who avoids business gatherings and goes off to Maine to make dulcimers. She's not an asset, but neither has she hindered his career. He's gone to the very top of the ladder."

"Maybe because she was down on the ground holding it for him," Piet said softly.

"You, my darling Piet, are a very wise man."

" 'Tis the season for wise men." He laughed and pulled into another overlook.

"You know, Piet," she said as they were nearing Stonefield. "I've been receiving garden catalogs all fall. Three spring ones last week. Could you have? How could you have?"

"I sent your name to a few catalog houses. I never asked myself why, but I know now, and you know, that it was because I hoped to lure you back to our gardens."

"You don't believe, then, that I was just pretending to love the gardens."

"No. I don't think I ever really believed that. I certainly don't believe it now that you've quit your job. How could anyone trade all of that money and prestige for a chance to dig weeds?"

"With you. Don't forget that you are the essential ingredient, my dearest Piet."

* * *

The road entering Stonefield was like the road leading home. Nothing had changed in the little town except that the gallery and the restaurant were closed for the winter; the people on the sidewalks were local people, some of whom she recognized.

Piet turned off Main Street into a narrow driveway that led to a small parking area behind the mustard-colored house. There was a back door, but he led her around to the front, which, like the back, had three windows upstairs and two windows and a door down.

"Some people call this a half-house and some a two-over-two. Early nineteenth century." He opened the lower lock with a heavy, old-fashioned key, and then the upper lock with a modern key.

Downstairs was a narrow hallway with a straight, narrow stairway. The front room was of no particular distinction; it contained a modern metal desk and a four-drawer file cabinet. In the back room were floor-to-ceiling bookshelves, rich paneling, and a desk as large and elegant as Mr. Spencer's.

She ran into Piet's arms. "It's magnificent. Look at that desk. Why would anyone leave it behind?"

"The old lawyer was forced out of town in a hurry."

"Why? Is there something . . . ?"

"He tried to cheat Emily when she came to claim the Darrow estate. Incidentally, they've had their baby, a boy named Peter after Peter Darrow. Back to the lawyer. He couldn't get the desk out without removing part of the wall, which is how he got it in."

"So I'm stuck with it and I'm glad. My clients—if and when I have some—will have to be impressed, maybe even awed, when they see this desk in this office."

A half-bath had been tucked in under the stairs. Upstairs were a full bath and two more rooms. The paper on the walls of the front room was light green with pink cabbage roses. As she stood riveted by its absolute hideousness, Piet reached up and pulled a strip of it from ceiling to floor. Meg found another loose strip and did likewise. In a few minutes they had pulled all of the paper from a narrow wall.

The wallpaper in the back room was dirty brown with stripes of faded flowers and blue bows. Unfortunately it appeared to be clinging tightly to the walls. In all the rooms, upstairs and down, were huge radiators, but the house was cold. She shivered.

"I turned off the heat except in the bathrooms," Piet said, pulling her into the shelter of his body. "I expect we could install a small kitchen, and rent this space, at least in the summer, maybe year round."

"Right." She turned to face him. "Now, let's talk business. How much did you pay for it? Mortgage? Interest rate? Insurance? I'll reimburse you as soon as I can arrange—"

"It's a present, Meg."

"No. I wouldn't allow it. No matter if it's in your name, or mine, or owned jointly, I will—"

"It's a present, Meg. Besides, it didn't cost much more than my new truck."

"But I couldn't accept—"

"Why couldn't you?" He scowled at her and walked around her and stomped down the stairs. He stopped at the bottom of the stairs and waited for her to join him. "You are too damned independent, Meg. I bought this house on speculation. I was speculating that you would come back and need an office. I bought it for you. Men—women too, I suppose—like to give things to those they love."

"I haven't received many presents, Piet. I don't know how to accept graciously."

"You say 'thank you very much' and then you kiss the giver." He took her in his arms.

Sometime later, she asked if she could move into the upstairs rooms in a few weeks.

"Here? You want to live here? What's wrong with my A-frame?"

She grinned. "I want to be the attorney for the people of this town, including the little old ladies who will need wills and tax advice. The appearance of propriety is important, darling."

He nodded, agreeing reluctantly. Then he grinned. "I felt terrible when we were mad at each other. I suppose that's why we have to wait to get married, to become acquainted with one another's foibles. I should have known how independent you are."

"And you? Do you like your independence, Piet?"

"Oh yes. And I like yours, too. It might be flattering if you couldn't make a decision without me, but it might also be burdensome."

"I have another foible you should know about."

"Confess."

"I like to eat, often. I'm hungry right now."

Later, they walked to Miss Pearce's house, rang the bell, and entered the garden room holding hands. The old lady looked up from the plant she was repotting and nodded silently while she studied their faces.

At last she spoke. "I'm glad to see you, girl. I'd hoped you'd choose gold over glitter. You two have gladdened an old lady's heart." She turned back to her work.

The next day Meg and Piet scraped the wallpaper from the upstairs rooms in the mustard-colored house and hung a big wreath on the front door.

Christmas was a kaleidoscope of joy. On the afternoon of the twenty-fourth, Piet and Meg drove through snow-covered hills and gaily lit villages to arrive in Brinton in time to hang the last strands of tinsel on the tree.

Pandemonium was the order of Christmas morning. Meg watched in wonder as paper and ribbons flew like dervishes about the room. Shouts and laughter and oohs and aahs drowned out recorded carols. When Piet lifted the book on Hudson River paintings from the wrappings, he ran his hand across the glossy cover and then kissed her soundly.

He gave her a copper-colored down-filled jacket. "It, and my love, will keep you warm during the cold winter ahead," he said, kissing her again.

Meg shivered with happiness.

Piet was loading the truck for their trip back to

Stonefield when Barry drew Meg into a corner of the kitchen and handed her a small flat package. "I've been saving this for you," he whispered.

Bewildered, she opened the package and stared down at an old photograph in a new frame. A thin young man sat on the ground under a large tree. He was smiling at the little girl in his lap. "Daddy and me." Meg sobbed as the tears that had floated and trickled all morning suddenly became a torrent. She had loved her father. Perhaps one day she would be able to forgive her mother. Barry held her in his arms, patting her back, until Piet returned.

"I like him," Barry whispered in her ear before he pushed her toward Piet. "Please get her out of here before we all drown," he said, laughing.

"I can see the headlines now," Piet said, as he put his arm around Meg and led her toward the door. "Family of five drowns in sister's tears. She doesn't seem capable of speech so I will have to act as her interpreter. Meg is one very happy woman who loves each one of you and thanks you all for everything."

He was right. Meg couldn't speak but she nodded vigorously.

Snow began to fall in luscious big flakes just as they entered Stonefield. They had a quiet dinner in front of the fireplace with Miss Pearce, who gave Meg amethyst earrings that had belonged to her grandmother.

When the old lady had gone to her room, Piet took a box from the mantel and handed it to Meg.

"More?" she asked, shaking her head. "I can't

take any more presents. I'm not accustomed to such riches. It's . . ."

"Shall I open the box?" Piet took it from her and lifted a carving from it. Two beavers from a single piece of wood. "As long as we both shall live," he said. "Like the beavers."

She lifted her lips to his.